Where Would You Fly & Other Magical Stories

Lillian Darnell

LOVING KINDNESS BOOKS

Reno, Nevada

Published by Loving Kindness Books
PO Box 19812, Reno, NV 89511
LovingKindnessBooks.com
WhereWouldYouFly.com

First Printing January 2018

"Printing/manufacturing information for this book may be found on the last
page"

The text of this book is set in Garamond.

Publisher's Cataloging-in-Publication Data
Darnell, Lillian, 2001-
Where would you fly and other magical stories / Lillian Darnell with cover
photo by Camilla Downs - 1st edition
Summary: A collection of original fairy tales, legends, short stories, and
poems written by Lillian Darnell, who has a chromosome deletion, 18p-,
written when she was between the ages of four and fifteen years old.
ISBN 978-0-9800568-3-9 (paperback)
1. Fairy tales. 2. Short Stories.
3. Poetry. I. Darnell, Lillian II. Title 398.21
LCCN 2017959406

Author, Lillian Darnell, copyright 2018, all rights reserved
Contributing Author, Camilla Downs, copyright 2018, all rights reserved
Principle Editor, Camilla Downs
Secondary Editor, Thomas Darnell
Secondary Editor, Lois Savin
Cover Design by Kate Raina
Cover Photography by Camilla Downs, copyright 2018, all rights reserved
Interior Layout and Graphics by Kate Raina
Interior Illustrations by Lillian Darnell, copyright 2018, all rights reserved
Interior Photography by Camilla Downs, copyright 2018, all rights reserved

<u>Praise For Where Would You Fly & Other Magical Stories:</u>

"You can't help but feel happy and be inspired while reading this book. Lillian's stories jump straight out of her heart and onto the pages in an authentic, innocent, and loving way. The world needs more positivity and happiness and her stories are bursting with both. Thank you Lillian!"

G. Brian Benson - *Award winning and Best-selling author, Actor and TEDx speaker*

"Let your imagination be taken away with Lillian Darnell's writings and allow yourself to be transported to places where anything is possible with love, joy and a touch of inspiration. This collection is born from a young woman with a unique perspective on how our world could be - immerse yourself and come, see the world through Lillian's eyes."

Dr. Veronica Wain - *Award winning filmmaker, Academic, Author, Disability Advocate*

"Great, awesome, and very amazing."

D.J. Svoboda - *Autistic Artist, Author, and Public Speaker*

"Although all of us who love fairies understand that children, with their vivid imaginations, are closer to magic than any of us, we all yearn to retain that childlike sense of wonder. Lillian Darnell's writings are a welcome reminder of what is possible when you dream big, and accept no limitations."

Grace Nuth - *Senior Editor - Faerie Magazine*

"It's like seeing the world with fresh and awakened eyes." - **Camilla Downs** - *Best-selling author, Mom, Nature photographer*

"Stories that are always fun to read."

Thomas A. Darnell - *Author and Philosopher*

1

This book is dedicated to my mother, Camilla Downs, for helping put together the book and for helping inspire me to write.

With Much Gratitude:

Special thanks to Camilla Downs, Thomas Darnell, and Kate Raina for helping put together this book. I'm grateful to Christine McBride and Robert Downs for supporting me.

Thank you to Patty Romano, Frank Romano, Rebecca Parker, Macy Miller, Katie Baker, Britney Lynn, Tanya Glass, Jillian Johnson, Ted Darnell, Mark Sogard, Heidi Hulspas, Abby Reed, Cierra Fudala, Brigitte Frost, and Alexa Waldmann.

Thank you to Brian Benson, Veronica Wain, D.J. Svobada, and Faerie Magazine for giving my book a review blurb.

Thank you to the authors of these books:

Mary Pope Osborne, Natalie Bryce, and Will Osborne - *The Magic Treehouse Series*

Daisy Meadows - *Rainbow Magic Series*

L.M. Montgomery - *Anne of Green Gables*

Helen Perelman - *The Candy Fairies Series*

Thanks to the creators, directors, actors, and actresses of these movies:

Barbie and the Diamond Castle

The Princess and the Frog

The Little Mermaid

The Little Mermaid 2

Sleeping Beauty

Frozen

TABLE OF CONTENTS

Melody the Dog

Sapphire and Topaz Mystery Solver

The Adventurous Pineapple Family

A Cat with Magic Powers

Where Would You Fly

Life as an Autumn Gold Apple

A Realistic World Beyond Your Eyes

A Friendship Between Four Types of Candy

Fruit Fashion

The Secret Place

Alsatian and His Family – An All Language Legend

Truthful Art: A Chinese Legend

The Myth of the Unusual Rainbow Decades

Witch Creation

Patty's Love and Lillian's Style

The Storm is Coming

The Bear Eats Bees

The Whale Who Wore Clothes

Never Sleep with Bears

The Cat Who Wore Glasses

Fun on the Farm

The Fantastic Idea

Spreading the Great Nature

The Big Day for Nature

What the Animals Saw

The Surprises

What the Guests Did at the Party

Notebook

Triple Poems

Shadows are Always There

Enchanted Egyptian Beauty

A Friendly Letter to Robert Frost

FORWARD

The pages you are about to experience are not typical fairy tales, adventures, and poems. They were written by a wonderful and unique human being, the kind who comes around only once in every 56,000 births. Her name is Lillian Darnell, and she is missing the short arm of her 18th chromosome. Written between the ages of four and fifteen, this book is a fulfillment of a promise I made to Lillian, who is now sixteen-years-old.

At the age of three, Lillian was delayed in more than three milestones, so her pediatrician referred us, and her, for in depth blood testing. She was diagnosed with a condition called 18p-. So began a different journey which I wrote about in my first book, *"D iz for Different - One Woman's Journey to Acceptance".*

You will find additional information regarding The Chromosome 18 Registry & Research Society in the back of this book.

The most inhibiting effect of 18p- for Lillian is her ability to communicate. She simply cannot articulate letter sounds the way the rest of us are accustomed to hearing them pronounced. This causes much of her speech to be unintelligible. Other ways in which the deletion has affected her are irrational fears, anxiety, sensory issues, balance issues, low pain tolerance, challenges with processing emotions and change, and difficulties with the proprioceptive system.

She and I learned the basics of sign language before she was even diagnosed so that we could communicate. I created small square magnets with pictures of everyday items and stuck them to the fridge. I also created a notebook with the same pictures. The sign language and pictures are what we used to communicate until she learned to spell and write.

When Lillian was in early elementary, the school provided a Dynavox for her to use for communication. In 2009, when Lillian was eight, a life changing app named Proloquo2Go was released that would revolutionize communication for those with articulation difficulties. With the help of my parents, I purchased Lillian an iPhone and the app. She used it for several years to enhance her spoken word when attempting to communicate. At the age of nine, Lillian chose to discontinue learning and using sign language.

A few years ago, Lillian tapered her use of the app and prefers to use the spoken word. Her articulation is still difficult to understand, yet this is her preferred method of communication. With patience and mindfulness, the person with whom she is speaking can eventually understand what she is saying.

Lillian began to read at an early age and has had a love of books since being an infant. She chose to sleep with books in her crib rather than stuffed animals, of which she never liked the feel. I sensed when Lillian was about six that she would benefit from an easy way to get the abundance of thoughts and words out of her imagination. Her grandfather, Robert Downs, gifted her a tiny, pink Asus computer for her birthday that year, and here we are with Lillian Darnell a published author!

Lillian has always had difficulty processing change. Any changes from what she expected produced unwanted emotions, and Lillian struggled letting herself feel these emotions. When puberty began, this intensified with deepening irrational fears and violent outbursts. The struggles she had with processing emotions led to the "Emotions with Animals" section of the book. It takes a detour into a period of time that Lillian and I were working together using mindfulness and emotional connection. It was her idea to write these as blog posts, pairing animals with certain emotions. She did her own research, asking for my input with the concluding tips section.

I describe the whole of these collected writings as a fictional anthology of Lillian's life and imagination to date. The imagination and creative process of one with a chromosome deletion and how she chooses to see the world. Some were written on paper prior to Lillian's use of a computer. Some were school work assignments or gifts to a family member. The rest were written as blog posts on an earlier blog, PinkElephantBooks.com, and Lillian's current blog, LillianDarnell.com. The stories and poems were mostly edited for spelling and grammar, yet the bulk of the stories will remain as she originally wrote and published them; including a few grammatical errors and made up words.

One other thing to note are the references to TLC or Team TLC. In the year 2009, I had a feeling I should think of a term for referring to our family; a term or name that would help instill a sense of cohesion and teamwork. That is when Team TLC was born. The T stands for Thomas, L stands for Lillian, and C stands for Camilla.

As Lillian's mother, I knew deep within that being an artist was to be her path. I have done my best to support her artistic endeavors. As you read, may you leave this reality behind and allow yourself to be blessed by taking a journey through Lillian's world.

Namasté,
Camilla Downs
Lillian's Blessed Mother

FAIRIES AND
PRINCESSES

SPARKLE: A SPARKLY LIFE AS A FAIRY PRINCESS

Once upon a time there lived two parents who wanted at least a daughter and a son. So one night, on September 13th, in the year 2000, a daughter was born at 9:00 p.m. Her name was Sparkle because her eyes sparkled like diamonds ever since she opened her eyes for the first time.

When Sparkle was four-years-old, her mother discovered that her daughter had a short arm chromosome deletion called 18p-; and her mother decided to find out as much possible about 18p-.

When Sparkle was five-years-old, her parents had a son on November 13th, in the year 2005. His name was Ocean because he had ocean colored eyes ever since he had opened his eyes for the first time.

When Sparkle was nine-years-old, she went to her first 18p- conference in Las Vegas, Nevada. She made two friends named Rainbow and Shimmer and she had a lot of fun at her first conference! Ever since then, she liked the conferences.

Sparkle had gotten books, clothes, homemade stuff, and other store bought stuff for Christmases to come. When she was fifteen-years-old, she got almost everything she wanted especially the laptop and telescope. She even got what she wanted for her birthday.

So far, they live happily ever after!

This story is a fantasy version of my life.

(Written January 2016 at 14-years-old)

FAIRYLAND ADVENTURES

Hey, there! I've created the Fairyland Adventure series for everyone (especially for fairy lovers to read.) This is the introduction of the series. Have fun reading the series!

June 3rd – (At Night)
That night Lilliana had a dream of a magical car wash and some colorful lights moving. She saw herself in her dream. It instantly disappeared that very night. She wondered what the dream had meant but she wanted to see the same dream again.

June 4th – (Morning)
Lilliana told her mother, Camille about the vision she saw the night before. Lilliana asked Camille if she had any idea what the dream meant.

June 7th – (Night)
After Lilliana saw the dream for three nights, she saw that the magical car wash was slowly transforming before her eyes.

June 10th – (Night)

That very night all of Fairyland appeared before her eyes. Lilliana instantly loved the place. So she went to ask the Fairy Queen about what to do to get into Fairyland and what she would need. The Fairy Queen had said that there will be a dressing room portal where Lilliana could change into her fairy outfit and wings. When Lilliana comes back, her clothes would be right where she had left them.

June 11th – (Night)

That night she checked out her amazing portal and she went to explore the place. That is how Fairyland came to be. Hope you enjoyed this fairyland introduction!

(Written May 2016 at 14-years-old)

FAIRY SHADOWS

Once there was a girl who dreamed of shadows in Fairyland. Her name was Lilliana. She was curious why the shadows were orange, pink, and many other colors. In Fairyland the shadows were very pretty and very stylish.

One day, she decided to live in Fairyland. So she packed everything she thought was necessary. After she was done packing, she headed to Fairyland.

When she arrived she began observing the colorful shadows. After a while, she went to ask the Shadow Fairy why the shadows were colored. The Shadow Fairy said, "I was experimenting with shadows. Everyone seemed to like the colorful shadows. So I left it that way."

Lilliana said, "That's amazing. Do you mind if I live in Fairyland?" The Shadow Fairy replied,

"Absolutely!" So Lilliana thanked the Shadow Fairy and went on her way.

Lilliana met a fairy named Samantha and they became the best of friends. Samantha actually referred Lilliana to Amal and Jessica. Lilliana said "It's nice to meet you Jessica and Amal."

Jessica and Samantha visited Lilliana a lot after that day. When Lilliana got to her preferred age, she started wanting Amal to visit with her. At first, she wanted Amal to come with Jessica and Samantha.

But after a while, Lilliana wanted Amal to come alone. As they visited more frequently, their friendship blossomed into love. One day, they went to the Fairyland telescope so Lilliana could see her home on earth.

Lilliana was surprised at how much the place changed. Lilliana yearned to go back. So Lilliana became the Sun Fairy and Lilliana could visit the Earth whenever she wished.

Amal asked Lilliana, "Will you marry me?" Of course she said Yes. So they got engaged. After a year, they planned a wedding. On June 21st, they got married. From this day forward, you can see them flying happily across the sky. Amal is the Sky Fairy. Sarah and Jessica worked as a Spring and Summer Fairy.

The End!

(Written April 2017 at 15-years-old)

PRINCESS BEAUTY

"Beauty is always in you, no matter what people say." - Princess Britney

This story is about a girl who wants to become a princess. Her life is changed in a way she'll never forget. Read more to find out what happens. I hope you enjoy!

Once there was a girl named Britney. She was always beautiful and kind; but she was lonely. You see, Britney's parents left for America when she was three-years-old and her friends left for Hawaii when she was five-years-old.

One day, Britney was in her garden thinking about how lovely it would be to be a princess. Suddenly, she heard her name being called and she wondered who it was. When she saw a maid with a scroll, she asked who is the maid and what is the scroll.

The maid said her name is Maiden Becca of England and the scroll is an invitation to the ball of England. When Becca left, Britney opened the scroll carefully. The scroll explained that Princess Lillian was too young to rule England, so Queen Camilla declared a ball to figure out who should be the temporary princess.

The invitation said to be there at 7:00 p.m. and to wear a gown or dress to the ball. Britney saw it was 6:30 p.m. and she went to find her beautiful sparkly rainbow gown with a ribbon around the hem and her matching sparkly rainbow tiara. The tiara was handmade by Britney herself.

About ten minutes later, Britney was ready for the ball. By 6:50 p.m., she saw a beautiful carriage. She stepped into the magnificent carriage and in five minutes they arrived.

As Britney walked into the castle, she tried to imagine what it would be like to live in the castle. Britney approached slowly to the ballroom, not sure what to expect. When Britney entered the ballroom she found herself looking down at royalty.

After she looked down at royalty, she slowly headed down shiny marble steps in a spiral. Everyone including the royal family looked in awe at Britney. She began to dance in slow graceful moves that impressed everyone.

She went to the table that had fruit punch. While there she started talking to Queen Camilla and King Camelot about how kind she was and how she wondered what being a princess was like.

When Queen Camilla finished talking, Britney politely grabbed a chocolate covered cherry. While Britney talked to Princess Lillian, Queen Camilla and King Camelot discussed whether

Britney should be the temporarily crowned princess or not.

After a few hours, Queen Camilla announced it was time to decide who would be the temporarily crowned princess. Queen Camilla began, "The crowned princess will be...," paused Queen Camilla for effect.

As a few seconds went by, Britney felt her heart beating with anxiousness. "Britney", said Queen Camilla. Britney couldn't believe what she had heard but she walked up to the thrones when she heard her name.

Queen Camilla said, "I now declare you Princess Britney of England. Would you like to make a speech, Princess Britney?" Britney responded with a polite, "Yes." Britney told the royalty and people who came to the ball that she was honored to be the princess of England, to tour the castle, and she would get to know everyone in the castle.

Britney ended her speech by saying, "Beauty is always in you, no matter what people say." By the time the ball was over, it was 11:00 p.m. and Britney thought she should get some rest before exploring the castle the next day. She easily found her bedroom.

The next morning, she woke up not knowing where she was. After a few seconds, Britney realized she was in a castle bedroom. Now that the sun was up, she could see the princess room.

When Britney stepped outside her bedroom door, she saw a note from Queen Camilla saying that breakfast was in the ballroom at 8:30 a.m. Britney looked at a nearby clock and the time was 7:30 a.m.

The note said she had a maid named Becca to help her get dressed. Britney would just ring the bell so the maid would hear it. She rang the bell with the sweetest movement.

Britney went to her bedroom and she saw Maiden Becca. Maiden Becca said as she dressed Britney, "Good Morning, Princess Britney. Congratulations on becoming a princess! I think you should walk to the dining room for breakfast."

Britney had said in response, "Good Morning, Maiden Becca! Thank you kindly. I will walk to the dining room after I take a quick glance in the mirror." Britney took a quick glance in the mirror and gasped.

Britney was wearing a sparkly striped rainbow dress with rosettes in her hair. She had indigo-rainbow shoes on her feet and a beautiful blue rainbow tiara on her head. Britney walked into the dining room carefully.

Britney watched how the royalty ate and she repeated the movement. After breakfast, Britney explored the castle and she met the people working inside the castle. Maiden Becca told her there was a royal garden in the courtyard which was through the doors.

When Maiden Becca said the word garden, Britney's face lit up with delight. When Britney saw the garden, she walked around exploring the garden until the birds sang. Britney saw a message from Queen Camilla saying royal lessons were to be in the royal gym.

Britney told herself that she would have to come back. So Britney went back to her bedroom and rung the bell again but this time Maiden Becca brought the royal tailor in to create a simple gym dress. Maiden Becca gave the sizing to the royal tailor.

Britney waited patiently for the royal tailor to get done with the dress. The simple dress was created just three seconds later. She left her room feeling amazed and headed to the royal gym.

Britney walked into the royal gym, not sure what to expect. She was surprised to find a tutor who had lived in the castle several years, and the tutor helped the past princesses and princes learn about royalty.

Britney was pleased to find the tutor was funny and shared a love of nature. Queen Camilla said Britney's royal lessons will begin on Thursdays. Britney was delighted she had Thursdays to look forward to.

During her royal lesson, Britney learned about yoga. After her royal lesson, she found a note from King Camelot. He said to meet in the ballroom for dancing lessons.

So Britney went to her bedroom to get dressed with help from Maiden Becca. After Maiden Becca finished dressing her, she went to the ballroom for dancing. She was surprised that the same tutor was there.

This time the tutor demonstrated dance moves for her. The tutor explained that yoga was related to dancing in a way. After her dance lesson, she found a note telling her lunch was ready. She quickly walked toward the dining room.

Before Britney could open the door to the dining room, she was greeted by Queen Camilla. Queen Camilla said Britney was doing great and that ruling lessons began tomorrow because she was doing a great job.

Maiden Becca was standing around and she offered to open the door for them. Queen Camilla and Princess Britney said it would be lovely. When they entered the door, Britney sat down to eat but she figured she should wait until everyone in the dining room was eating.

At 12:15 p.m. everyone was eating, including Britney. After lunch there were no notes so she decided to go back to the garden again. This time she looked around the garden until she saw a few butterflies and peacocks and she sang to them.

The peacocks and butterflies didn't want Britney to go when she saw the note from Queen Camilla. She went to Queen Camilla's throne room. The first thing Queen Camilla asked was how was her day.

Britney responded by saying her day was great. The next thing Queen Camilla asked was what was her favorite part of the day. Britney said, "Going out to the garden."

Queen Camilla asked, "Is there anything else you'd like to improve?" Britney had told Queen Camilla that she thought her singing needed to be improved. Before Britney left, Queen Camilla told her that dinner would be around 6:15 p.m.

Queen Camilla had also told Britney that she had the rest of the day to do whatever she wished. So Britney headed toward Maiden Becca and asked her if there were any different gardens.

Maiden Becca said there was a butterfly garden, bird garden, and flower garden.

Britney thought she would go to the butterfly garden. Maiden Becca told her how to get to the butterfly garden. When Britney opened the door, she was amazed to see so many butterflies. So she walked around humming to the butterflies. Again when she left to go look for the bird garden, the butterflies didn't want her to leave.

Britney found the bird garden easily. She was impressed with how many birds were there. As she walked in the garden, she tweeted, chirped, hooted, and cooed with a sweet melody. Once again, the birds didn't want her to go when she went to the flower garden.

Britney found the flower garden door. Britney thought that the flower garden looked identical to the main garden but she went in anyway.

She sang again with a lilt in her voice and the birds and butterflies came to her. This time, the birds sang along while the butterflies fluttered their wings to the tune. The birds and butterflies didn't want Britney to go.

Britney knew she had to get ready for dinner. This time as Britney walked, she saw King Camelot walking toward her. When King Camelot approached, he asked how Britney liked living here and he also said that Princess Lillian enjoys Britney's company.

Britney said, "I enjoy living here, Your Majesty. I'm glad that Princess Lillian enjoys my company." The King held the door open for Britney. When Britney sat down, she noticed everyone but King Camelot eating.

So Britney determined she should eat. Britney also made a mental note to ask the tutor what is the proper way to eat at a castle. When she was heading out of the dining room, she saw Maid Macy in the royal library cleaning the books.

Britney decided she would go into the library to read instead of going back to the garden. She asked Maid Macy if she had any book recommendations. Maid Macy grabbed a book called the *"Sunshine Beauty"* by F. Lien.

Maid Macy asked her if the book sounded good. Britney told her it sounded great to her.

It was getting late so Britney took the book with her to bed. She read a little before she turned off her royal lamp.

Britney lay in the dark thinking about the busy day ahead of her. After a while, she drifted to sleep. When she woke up, it was morning again. She got up to ring the bell to get Maiden Becca's attention.

Instantly, Maiden Becca came and dressed her. This time after Maiden Becca dressed her, Britney had more time to talk to Maiden Becca because Britney woke up a little earlier. Britney talked about her old home and it's garden.

Maiden Becca told her about her pets and her books. Maiden Becca also told her that she'd often go to the royal library. Britney showed her the *"Sunshine Beauty"* book. After a little while though, Britney had to get to the dining room.

As Britney headed to the dining room, Britney stopped by the royal library to see if Maid Macy was there. Britney didn't see Maid Macy so she went on her way to the dining room. Surprisingly, she got to the dining room early.

Britney looked around the dining room and saw pictures of past Queens and Kings of England. Finally, it was 7:00 a.m. and Queen Camilla walked in with King Camelot. The maids who ate breakfast with them walked in also.

They were all surprised to see Princess Britney sitting in her chair looking around the dining room. Britney noticed the surprised looks of Queen Camilla, King Camelot, and the maids.

Britney explained that she hadn't looked around in the dining room fully. Queen Camilla said, "I'm okay with that, Britney." The King and maids agreed with Queen Camilla.

They all began to eat breakfast together and nothing was heard but eating sounds. After breakfast, she went to have a ruling lesson with the tutor. Before they started on the ruling lesson though, Britney remembered to ask what is the proper way to eat at a castle. The tutor said, "That is a big question with a short answer. I have noticed they don't wait for everyone to start eating and they eat quietly as a mouse."

So the tutor began the ruling lesson. Britney learned the proper way to wave and speak to crowds of people. After she left the tutor, she decided to go to the flower garden to read. Britney thought she should read out loud to the animals.

So she began to read out loud until she had to leave. The animals didn't want Britney to go. Britney promised she'd bring food for them soon.

Next, Britney went to her royal music lesson in the music room. After she left the music room, she went directly to the library to check for Maid Macy. Britney saw Maid Macy in the library.

Britney immediately asked Maid Macy about seeing Maiden Becca. Maid Macy said she'd seen Maiden Becca several times in the library. After she left the library, she went to get lunch because she was starving.

The lunch today was chip chicken and bacon wrapped pork. Britney was delighted to be treated with yummy delicacies. After lunch, she went to her dancing lesson. She practiced basic ballet moves.

After Britney was done in the ballroom, she went to the flower garden and, like she promised, she brought food with her. After she left the garden, she went to talk to Queen Camilla about singing lessons.

Queen Camilla told her that her singing was beautiful, but it needed more tune. After Britney left the throne room, she went to her first singing lesson. She learned basic tips of singing a better tune and how to soothe her throat for singing.

After the singing lesson, Britney went to the royal gym to swim until dinner. At dinner, she began thinking about writing a story. After dinner, she went to her bedroom to take notes of her ideas.

After she finished her story ideas, she rang the bell for Maiden Becca. Instantly, Maiden Becca came. Britney asked Maiden Becca if she knew any story starters.

Maiden Becca said she did and told her the tips. After Maiden Becca left, Britney started writing the first draft of a story. Shortly after she had finished writing her chapter, she sat in her bed reading.

After reading two chapters though, Britney felt tired, so she turned off the lamp and went to sleep. When Britney woke the next morning, something seemed wrong but she didn't know what. So she rang the bell like she usually would.

Maiden Becca didn't come so Britney looked in the maid book for how many rings would summon Maid Macy. The book said to do only two rings. Instantly, Maid Macy came. Maid Macy dressed Britney quickly.

After Maid Macy dressed Britney, Britney asked where was Maiden Becca. Maid Macy responded that Maiden Becca wasn't feeling good. Maid Macy and Britney walked to the dining room for breakfast.

When Queen Camilla came in, Maid Macy and Britney walked over to Queen Camilla to ask if they could announce that Maiden Becca was sick. Queen Camilla said, "Alright."

After Maid Macy and Britney announced that Maiden Becca was sick, they ate and then went to see Maiden Becca. Maiden Becca who had looked so cheerful last night looked pale and sad.

Britney went to her singing lesson first that morning. Britney sang with a bit of tune but she was too worried about Maiden Becca. After her singing lesson, she went to see Maiden Becca again.

The royal doctor reported that Maiden Becca was expecting a baby. Britney raced to the maid headquarters to tell the maids.

The maids were impressed including Maid Macy. The maids and Britney went to tell King Camelot and Queen Camilla together. Queen Camilla seemed surprised and relieved when she heard the news.

King Camelot seemed anxious and excited. After the maids and Britney left the throne room, Britney went to her dance lesson.

Britney danced her emotions out freely. Her tutor was amazed at how freely she danced when she let out her emotions.

The tutor asked Britney why it was so easy for her. Britney told the tutor about the news and the tutor was pleased. After Britney's dancing lesson, she went to sing in the bird garden. Britney sang her emotions.

The animals had gotten used to Britney leaving them. After Britney left the garden, she went to her music lesson. The tutor taught her a new tune on the ukulele and she did it perfectly.

After Britney was done with her music lesson, she went to see Maiden Becca. Britney was delighted to see Maiden Becca awake. Britney greeted her with a good morning and Maiden Becca told her good morning in a quiet voice.

Maiden Becca slowly fell asleep again so Britney left the room. Britney headed to her bedroom and she suspected something strange. Britney began writing the clues. She got the answer for the question. The tutor was Maiden Becca's husband.

Britney left to talk to Queen Camilla. Britney told Queen Camilla what she'd discovered. Queen Camilla looked confused and asked for the tutor. Queen Camilla asked, "Is it true that you are Maiden Becca's husband?" The tutor responded, "Yes."

The tutor told Britney that she was a clever girl. After meeting with Queen Camilla, Britney went to see Maiden Becca but this time the doctor was there. The doctor told Britney that the baby was almost fully grown and that the baby would come out on Thursday. Britney had the whole afternoon to do whatever she pleased.

Britney went to her room to work on her story. After Britney finished writing the second chapter, dinner was ready. She walked into the dining room and ate dinner. After she ate dinner, she went back to her bedroom to write the third chapter.

The third chapter was about a princess. After she finished her third chapter, Britney went to the dining room to eat dinner. Britney told Queen Camilla about when Maiden Becca's baby was due.

Queen Camilla was amazed. The queen told Britney she could go visit Maiden Becca anytime from that point forward. After dinner, Britney went to the flower garden to watch the sun set and pick flowers.

The flowers she picked were lavender, rose, lilies, daffodils, dandelions, and more. After Britney was done picking flowers, she went to the royal craft room to spruce up the flowers.

After Britney finished sprucing the flowers, she did a three second portrait in full color of the flowers. She went to Maiden Becca to give her the flowers.

This time, Maiden Becca was awake. So Britney asked, "Do you feel well enough to tell me about how you married the tutor? If the story is too long, you could just tell the story slowly. I could ask the tutor if you don't feel well enough."

Maiden Becca said, "I think I feel well enough to tell you." So Maiden Becca told Britney about how the tutor and Maiden Becca met. Maiden Becca told her that they met in

Greenland and how Maiden Becca had worked as a gardener in the Kingdom of Luna.

After Maiden Becca said she was too sleepy to continue the story, Britney headed to her room to work on her story. After she finished her fourth chapter, she got into bed and read three chapters more of her book because she had more time tonight.

After Britney finished reading, she turned off the light and lay awake thinking how much excitement there had been Saturday. The next morning, Britney woke up and realized today was Sunday.

Britney found Queen Camilla was in the throne room so she went to the throne room to ask if she had almost the whole day off and whether she had to go to church. "Yes, you have almost all day off," said Queen Camilla. "You do have church lessons in the royal library every Sunday. You could even pray for Maiden Becca," added Queen Camilla.

Britney told Queen Camilla that she would like to pray for Maiden Becca. She went to her church lesson just after breakfast. The royal preacher read part of the Bible and then the royal preacher announced it was praying time.

Britney prayed for Maiden Becca like she said she would. She also prayed for the tutor and the other maids. After the church lesson, she went to see Maiden Becca. Once again, the royal doctor was there.

The royal doctor asked if Britney wanted to feel Maiden Becca's stomach. She said, "Yes." Britney instantly put her hand on Maiden Becca's stomach and she felt a kick come from inside Maiden Becca's stomach.

Britney asked if that was the baby kicking Maiden Becca's stomach. The royal doctor chuckled and answered, "Yes." Britney went to tell the ladies in waiting about the baby so they could tell Queen Camilla.

Queen Camilla was impressed by the update. After Britney left the throne room, she went to write another chapter of her book. Britney thought she was so lucky to get story tips from Maiden Becca before they found out that Maiden Becca was expecting a baby.

After Britney had finished writing three chapters of her book, she read a little bit of the book that Maid Macy had given her. After she finished reading, she realized she was hungry. So Britney went to look at the clock to see if it was close to lunch.

The clock said 12:15 p.m. and Britney knew that lunch was over. Luckily, she found Queen Camilla heading out of the dining room. Britney explained she had accidentally missed lunch.

Queen Camilla suggested Britney go to the dining room to see if the food was still out. Surprisingly, the food was still out and almost everyone was still sitting. So Britney started eating lunch because she was starving.

Maid Macy told Britney that she'd received more news about Maiden Becca's baby while Britney ate her lunch. Maid Macy told her that the baby was to be a baby girl. After Maid Macy left, she ate quickly so she could go see Maiden Becca.

As Britney walked into the door, she saw the doctor again. Britney asked what the doctor was doing and the doctor told her that she was helping examine the stomach to help guess how much the baby would weigh.

After Britney responded to the royal doctor, she left Maiden Becca and the doctor. She went to the flower garden to think of how crazy her past week had been. She couldn't believe that just last week she was at her cottage in her garden.

After Britney was in the flower garden, she went to have dinner with the royal family. After dinner, Britney went to see Maiden Becca again. The royal doctor said the baby might come out on Tuesday which was earlier than expected.

After the royal doctor left, she talked to Maiden Becca about how crazy her previous week had been. Maiden Becca nodded to show she agreed about how crazy the previous week had been. After Britney left Maiden Becca, she went to her room to write the next to last chapter of the book she was writing.

Then Britney read a little more in the book she was reading. After Britney read, she went to tell Queen Camilla and King Camelot about the baby being born on Tuesday instead of Thursday.

When Britney told Queen Camilla and King Camelot, they were surprised and called Princess Lillian into the royal throne room. After Princess Lillian was told about the news, she also looked surprised.

Queen Camilla, King Camelot, and Princess Lillian suggested they try to find a good name for a baby girl just in case Maiden Becca needed help choosing a name. "Can you check with the royal tutor and Maiden Becca to see what Maiden Becca's plan is after she has her baby?" asked King Camelot.

Britney said, "I'd be glad to check with the royal tutor and Maiden Becca to see what the plan is after her baby is born." So Britney went to find the royal tutor to see if he knew what was Maiden Becca's plan.

When Britney found him, she asked him if he knew Maiden Becca's plan. He responded that he knew. He told her that her plan was to still work as a part-time maid. Britney was relieved and then asked what was his plan.

The royal tutor told Britney that he was still going to be a full-time tutor for the royalties. Britney went to Queen Camilla to tell her about Maiden Becca's plan. Queen Camilla called Maid Macy into the royal throne room to tell her that she would be a part-time maid for Maiden Becca.

After Britney left, she went to her room to sleep. She could hardly wait to see what was in store for Monday. On Monday morning, she woke up excited because the baby girl would be due Tuesday.

Britney called Maid Macy to help her get dressed and she went to see Maiden Becca. The royal doctor was there again and the doctor told her she was in contractions.

Britney was concerned but she went to get Queen Camilla and King Camelot. Britney urged Maiden Becca to push a little for a few minutes. After she left, she went to eat breakfast.

Britney went to the bird garden to sing to help her feel better. She also went to read and write in her room before lunch. She had herbal chicken nuggets with curly fries, waffle fries, and smiley face fries for lunch.

Britney was glad to have something yummy to eat on such an important day. After she finished her yummy meal, she went to talk to Queen Camilla. After she'd talked to Queen Camilla, she went to find Maid Macy to talk to her.

Britney and Maid Macy talked until dinner time. At dinner, she wondered how Maiden Becca was doing. After dinner, she went to see Maiden Becca. She asked the doctor how Maiden Becca was doing.

The royal doctor told Britney that Maiden Becca was okay. After the visit to Maiden Becca, she decided to go to bed a little early so she could be awake in case the baby came in the morning. Of course, Britney still wrote her story and read a little in bed before going to sleep. On Tuesday morning, she quickly rang the bell to tell Maid Macy to dress her. After she dressed, she went to see Maiden Becca.

Britney could already see the baby's feet sticking out. She asked the royal doctor if she had time to devour her breakfast and share the news to Queen Camilla and King Camelot. The royal doctor told her that Britney had enough time to eat her breakfast and tell Queen Camilla. So she went by Queen Camilla's royal throne room to share the news.

Britney told Queen Camilla to pass the news to King Camelot and the other royalty. So she went to eat a waffle topped with fruit on it for breakfast and hurried back to the royal nursery room where everyone was quietly watching.

Soon, Britney could see the baby's belly. Shortly after, she could see the head. Once the baby was out, the royal doctor wrapped it in a special blanket. The royal doctor let Maiden Becca hold the baby. Maiden Becca declared the name to be Katie.

The royal tutor was relieved to see the baby girl. So as the year went by, Princess Lillian grew into a wise 10-year-old child. Meanwhile, Katie grew and talked, as well as walked by the time the year was over.

As for Britney, she resumed her studying and lessons. Britney still found time to read, sing, write, and walk in the gardens. As promised, Maiden Becca returned to her maid duty for the part-time maid job.

As eight more years passed, everything was normal. Katie was a talented nine-year-old at the time. Queen Camilla and King Camelot talked about getting Princess Lillian ready to rule.

Britney was finally ready for her final test as a temporary princess. After Britney succeeded, Queen Camilla and King Camelot had a surprise for Britney.

The surprise was a plane ticket to take Britney to see her parents in America and to see her friends in Hawaii. Britney was excited but she asked if she could still come visit. Queen Camilla and King Camelot said, "Yes, you may."

Of course, Britney went home to her beautiful cottage for a few days before her trip. After three days past, she flew on a special plane to America to see her parents. She was excited.

Britney recognized her parents immediately as she stepped outside the airport. Her parents ran over and said, "Wow, Britney. You have gotten tall and have grown up." So she explained how she got to America.

Britney stayed for a few days to know how life was in America. She left America by boat to travel to Hawaii. She immediately recognized her friends the moment she stepped off the boat.

Britney's friends ran over to Britney and said, "Wow, you look amazing, Britney! It's so great to see you again!" So Britney stayed a little while to see what life was like in Hawaii. Soon she had to go back home though.

Britney hoped to see her parents and friends again soon. Many years later, her friends and parents came to visit her. They had the most fun together before heading back to the United States of America.

A few years later, Britney met a man named Mark and fell in love. They married nine years later. After that, she had three babies. Their names were Heidi, Abby, and Sierra. They all lived happily ever after.

The End!

(Written April 2017 at 15-years-old)

ANGEL ISLAND

This story is about an island near Fairyland.

Once upon a time, there lived a fairy who was curious about the island. Her name was Angelica.

One day she decided to visit this mysterious island, but she knew that she would have to ask her fairy parents. When Angelica asked her fairy parents, her fairy parents said she could go.

So Angelica went to pack for the trip. After she packed, she decided to get started on her trip.

About five hours later, she reached her destination. The island had nothing on it. She decided to name it "The Island of Curiosity."

Angelica had a very good idea. So she flew home and left her belongings on the island.

She told her fairy parents the good idea. Her fairy parents agreed that it was a good idea. The idea was to bring all angels to the island.

Angelica would stay there in charge of the angels. Her fairy parents disliked the name chosen for the island. Angelica suggested "Angel Island" and her fairy parents really liked the name. It made sense also.

So Angelica went back with all the angels to the island. As the years past, the angels grew a lot and so did the island. It was no longer an island. It had become a Fairyland city. To this day, guardian angels and other angels live there with kind Angelica.

People who pass away choose to go to Angel Island or somewhere else. This is the end of the story.

(Written March 2017 at 15-years-old)

RAINBOW LOVE

This story is about rainbows and love. I hope you enjoy!

Once there lived two rainbows who didn't want to separate for the love of nature. Their names were Candy Rainbow and Princess Rainbow. One day, Candy Rainbow was accidentally separated from Princess. What they didn't know was that the Nature fairy had split them in half.

Candy desperately looked for Princess but there was no sign of her. Meanwhile, Princess was where Candy wasn't. She was anxious to find him but the Nature fairy wouldn't let her. Candy asked the Nature fairy about Princess. The fairy said, "No, I haven't seen her. I didn't separate you."

Candy thought the fairy was being suspicious. Princess started suspecting the fairy. After a year passed, they accidentally ran into each other. When the fairy found out, she was furious.

The fairy decided to put Princess invisible so she couldn't be seen when they bumped into each other. Candy tried to explain to the Nature fairy that rainbow magic was more powerful than fairy magic. Since the nature fairy wouldn't listen, Candy decided to show her what he tried to explain.

His plan was to use his magic and power to get Princess out of the invisible world. So when Princess saw he was stretching out to use his power, she decided to reach over and touch his stretched arc. Candy felt lighter somehow but he didn't know how.

Suddenly the invisible spell broke. The fairy was shocked at what happened and the fairy had to vanish. "It was me who helped you, Candy", said Princess softly. "Thank you, Princess!" and the rainbows' love was returned.

Princess thought if people saw them, it would be easier to have one rainbow be invisible. Princess decided to go invisible but Candy was able to see her. Every once in a while, Princess appeared behind Candy. That is why some people see double or triple rainbows.

(Written June 2016 at 14-years-old)

A VIEW OF A PRINCESS LIFE

You're about to enter a princess's life at her birth.

There once lived Queen Lilliana and King Topaz who yearned to have a child (specifically a daughter). Eventually, the Queen had a baby girl and the King and the Queen were very happy. They had a christening baby shower party and everyone in the kingdom came.

Everyone watched the queen name the baby. The queen had selected Melody as her name. When Melody was one-year-old, she talked like a princess should talk.

She was three-years-old when she learned to walk like a princess. She was five-years-old when she was crowned. She began to study at age seven. She got a new bed at nine-years-old.

She started washing her hair at eleven-years-old. She started brushing her hair at thirteen-years-old. She started getting dressed at age fifteen. She then started liking young princes at school during her sixteenth year.

She started getting boyfriends in her seventeenth year. She started dates with boys in her eighteenth year. She found the perfect boy to marry in her nineteenth year. She planned the wedding in her twentieth year.

She got married in her twenty-first year. She had babies in her twenty-second year. In the twenty-third year, she went to work.

In her twenty-fourth year, her husband died. In her twenty-fifth year, she became ill. In her twenty-sixth year, she died; but her parents still remember her.

So to remember her, they built a statue, made a speech, a museum, some art, some pictures, and some books. Her parents died shortly after all that was done. Her children took her place on the throne.

Nobody forgot her. When they died, they joined her so she didn't get lonely.

There's a lesson; and the lesson is you should always honor someone after they die especially if that person is special.

(Written May 2015 at 13-years-old)

FAIRIES OF JOY

Once upon a time there were twelve fairies who lived in a fairy academy that was built in 2003.

"Hello. My name is Joyce, but you can call me Joy for short," said Joy. "Hi there. My name is Blue," mumbled Blue. "Hi, my name is Fuschia, but please call me Alexa," giggled Alexa. "Hey. My name is Violet, but please do call me Violetta," blurted Violetta. "Howdy. My name is Red," murmured Red. "Hi, my name is Orange, but call me Oran and meet Yellow, Green, Purple, Pink, Lilac, and Lavender."

There was a fairy challenge one day near Christmas and fairy queen Joy asked them to bring a Christmas tree that is mini sized. So, the fairies thought and thought. Violetta thought that they should go to a human world.

Then, three minutes later they headed off to a human world. They arrived just in time for Christmas! The End.

(Written December 2014 at 13-years-old)

FAIRIES IN THE ROSES

There once was a rose bush full of fairies. The roses used to be the fairies home. Then suddenly there was a large creature creeping into the roses. It scared the fairies away.

Then the fairies came back the next day and looked at the damage the creature had done. They decided to move to the land called The Fairyland Queenland. Once they got settled they never went near the rose bush again.

Meanwhile, the creatures had the roses to themselves. The fairies never liked honey; even honey rolls. They tell secrets to each other. The fairies rarely liked boy fairies whom were so smart.

If you listen to a rose you just might hear a fairy whisper. The fairies never were friends with the creature and its family. They had learned their lesson that day.

The fairies had gathered roses while being sneaky and that was their rule. That's why you never see them during the day.

(Written April 2014 at 12-years-old)

THE FLYING UNICORNS CREATE A RAINBOW

The unicorns weren't always flying. One day one of the unicorns found a flying powder and they started flying! Shortly after they found a rainbow can in the sky. They painted rainbows in the sky.

But one day they couldn't fly in the sky. Suddenly they found a clue and they were off to find their powers.

The people began wondering what happened to the unicorns. The delivery person had come out of nowhere and said that the unicorns lost their powers.

Some of the people began murmuring, "Terrible." They decided to help them. When they got there, the unicorns explained everything.

They finally found the final clue along with their powers; as well as who put them there.

The unicorns discovered that it was the small creatures. After that, they showed no one their powers. They kept secret all the time.

(Written April 2014 at 12-years-old)

MY FAVORITE FAIRY FACTS

"Raindrops are like fairy whispers." -Unknown

"When the wind blows a soft breeze, if you listen hard enough, you'll hear fairies giggling." - Lillian Darnell

"When the first baby laughed for the first time, the laugh broke into a thousand pieces and they all went skipping about, and that was the beginning of fairies. And now when every new baby is born its first laugh becomes a fairy. So if you believe that you are a fairy, you'll be a fairy for any boy, girl, or adult to discover

Fairyland." - From the book *"Peter Pan"* by J.M. Barrie

"Dream deep into your loveable dreamland where every fairy earns her peace." – Lillian Darnell

"When a flower starts to dance in the wind, a fairy is in it."- Thomas Darnell

"If you hear the rain tip-tapping, that's the fairies dancing." - Lillian Darnell

(Written January 2014 at 12-years-old)

CONVERSATION WITH QUEEN VIOLETA AND PRINCESS ARIELLA (ARIEL)

Lillian Darnell: Hi there! Who am I talking to today? I'm so curious! Bless me!

Princess Violeta: Hello, my name is Violeta but most people call me Violet. I will call Mother. "Mother! Mother!"

Queen Ariella: "What is it, honey?" Oh, hello. Most people call me Ariel instead of Ariella.

Lillian: Why, how pleasant to meet you!! I'll call your daughter Violet; and you Ariel.

Violet: Let's get to know each other, Lillian. What is your favorite color? Mine is mint green.

Ariel: That's a nice question, Violet! What is your favorite animal? Mine is a unicorn!

Lillian: Every shade of blue is my favorite

color and my favorite animal is fish.

Violet: How old are you? I'm eleven-years-old. What grade are you in? I'm in second grade.

Ariel: What is your teacher? Violet's teacher is Miss Maned. What school do you go to? Violet's school is Aryana.

Lillian: I'm twelve-years-old and I'm in fifth grade. My teacher is Mrs. Brigitte. My school is High Desert Montessori. Bye bye. I have to get ready for bed.

Violet: Bye. See you around.

Ariel: Bye: Hope to see you again.

(Written November 2013 at 12-years-old)

FAIRY TED

Once upon a time there was a fairy named Ted and he lived with Uncle Duke.

One day he asked, "Why do fairies fly"?

Well, they like to fly.

The End

(Written June 2010 at 8-years-old)

EMOTIONS AND FEELINGS

EMOTIONS WITH ANIMALS

WISE TORTOISE AND SHY TURTLES

Hey, everyone! Welcome to "Emotions With Animals." This edition is in honor of water. This edition includes tortoises and freshwater turtles. Let's begin!

Wise tortoises live longer than average humans. So it makes them seem wise. Wise people have many experiences. They also meditate.

How To Be Wise:

- Know that you are wise from the heart.
- Help people. (This might make you feel and be wise.)

Shy turtles are scared of humans. So if you see one, you might be in luck. Turtles can be so shy that if you make any noise they'll just go back underwater.

Shy people stutter, blush, shake, become breathless, or speechless. Shy people might rarely talk. When they do talk, they might be so nervous that they stutter.

How To Avoid Being Shy:

- Overcoming your shyness will take practice.
- Take slow, steady steps forward. Going slow is okay, but be sure to go forward.
- Build confidence by taking one small forward step at a time.
- It's okay to feel awkward. It happens to everyone.
- Know you can do it.
- Be true to yourself.
- Pay attention to the thoughts you are having when you're experiencing shyness.
- Remind yourself that no one can see the butterflies in your stomach.
- Take deep breaths.
- Have sips of water. (This is healthy).

I hope you enjoyed this edition of "Emotions with Animals."

(Written August 2016 at 14-years-old)

HYPER BEAVERS

Hey, everyone! Welcome back to "Emotions With Animals". The emotion is hyper and the animal is beaver.

Beavers are hyper because most beavers are nocturnal. They get really hyper when loud noise scares them away.

People are hyper for several reasons. For example, sugar can make you hyper. They can also get too excited or anxious and that can result in being hyper.

How to Avoid Being Hyper:

- Connect with the hyper-ness.
- Take deep breaths.
- Practice meditation.
- Practice mindfulness.

(Written July 2016 at 14-years-old)

CALM MONARCH BUTTERFLIES

This edition of "Emotions With Animals" is in honor of a monarch butterfly flying so close to my head and my home. I hope you enjoy!

Monarch butterflies are calm when they're flying. They might also be calmer after they eat some monarch butterfly friendly plants.

When you or someone else is calm, you will feel a lot better. You will be more confident and relaxed. You will be happy, mindful, grateful, thankful, and joyful.

Take a moment to read this quote. If you want to, share it with family, friends, and relatives.

"Holding on to anger is like grasping a hot coal with the intent of throwing it at someone else; you are the one who gets burned." — Buddha

How To Be Calm:

- If you have anger: You should talk it out with someone you trust.
- If you have sadness: It's okay to be sad.
- If you have jealousy: Go to "Emotions With Animals: Jealous Parrots" to find what to do.
- If you have mischief: Go to "Emotions With Animals: Mischievous Pelicans" to find out what to do.
- Repeat Om Shanti Om. It's a mantra.
- Take a deep breath. Step outside for a moment.
- Draw or write.
- Go for a walk.
- Connect with whatever feeling that is making you feel not calm.
- Meditate.

I hope you enjoyed.

(Written June 2016 at 14-years-old)

LOVE AS CHIMPANZEES

Chimp love is almost like person love. They kiss, embrace, hug, talk, and groom. Are you wondering how much chimps are like people?

People love is basically kissing, hugging, talking, kind teasing, and living together. If you're a kid, it's usually a bit different than your parents. They will tuck you in, brush your hair, brush your teeth, floss your teeth, help take your clothes off, read to you, and help put on clothes.

How To Feel (or Be) Loved:

- Have meaningful conversations.
- You can do this with anyone at almost any time simply by asking about the other person, and listening to what they say.
- Open yourself to love.
- Change your beliefs about the world and love.

- If you tell yourself that people don't care, you'll put that energy into the world, and will get what you are telling yourself.
- If you tell yourself you'll never experience love, you'll block the flow of love.
- Remind yourself that: There's a lot of love in the world, there's plenty to go around, you deserve it, and it's coming to you every day.
- Love Yourself. Don't say judgmental things or say bad things about yourself.

(Written June 2016 at 14-years-old)

FEARFUL FISH

Fearful fish look into a mirror or reflection. Depending on the type of fish they may quarrel with their reflection. Some fish don't see well.

Fearful people can get hurt backs, stubbornness, dizziness, and more. Being fearful can be dangerous if you're not careful.

How To Be Fearless:

- Aware: Notice when you experience feelings of fear.
- Remind: Next time you notice the fear inside you, remind yourself that it's all in your mind and that most fears never happen.
- Ask: Ask yourself, "What's the worst thing that can happen if I do this?"
- Write: Write down a few ways to deal with the worst case scenario.
- Fearful: It's okay to be fearful.
- Thinking: The thoughts you are having might be keeping you from being fearless.
- Feelings: Your emotions might also keep you from being fearless. Notice your thoughts and ask yourself, "Is that true?" Physically feel the feeling.
- Patient: Be patient with yourself.
- Quiet: Be quiet and still. Saying to yourself you will progress through your fears.

(Written June 2016 at 14-years-old)

MISCHIEVOUS PELICANS

Mischievous pelicans eat fish with their beak with their see-through pouch open. Pelicans will look silly mischievous.

Mischievous people giggle nervously. If you ask someone "Are you hiding something?" and they might reply no to you. Be careful not to get mischievous yourself!

How To Not Be Mischievous:
- Channel Mischief: Channel your mischief into curiosity for things.

- Transform: Transform your mischief into a learning experience to keep from doing something dangerous or get you in trouble.
- Connecting: Connect with the feeling that comes with feeling mischievous. After you finish connecting with it, go for a walk in nature, or anything that will channel the mischief to something.

(Written May 2016 at 14-years-old)

GRACEFUL SWANS

Swans gracefully float across wetlands, lakes, ponds, and seas. Swans are calm most of the time. Most swans gracefully fly in hibernation season in search for warm water.

Graceful people can float in pools and beaches. People can be calm sometimes. People can walk, swim, play, smile, stand, and sit gracefully.

How To Be Graceful:

- Living: Live in a place full of kindness, courage, love, non-resistance and acceptance.
- Sleep: Knowing that you're loved helps you to go to sleep gracefully.
- Connecting With Emotions: It will make you feel graceful afterward.
- Responding: Respond with love.

(Written May 2016 at 14-years-old)

JEALOUS PARROTS

Jealous parrots might fan their tails and chatter loudly. The parrots might screech. The parrots might even try to scratch or bite a new animal. Occasionally, jealous parrots turn their feelings inward and start pulling out their own feathers.

Jealous people might find a way to get away from you. The jealous people might be thinking, "I wish I had that" or "I really want that" instead of being grateful for what they have. If you aren't careful enough, you might get jealous and pack the jealousness deep into your body and cause pain and difficulty.

How To Stop The Jealousy:

- Telling the Truth: Telling the person that you were jealous can make you feel a lot better. Take the time to talk about it with the person and see why they may be feeling the way they feel.
- Letting Go: It may seem hard but you'll feel better after. Let go of the cause of the jealousy.
- Make a list of things for which you are grateful. This will make you feel better.
- Go observe nature in silence. Observe the birds, ducks, geese, trees, flowers, and leaves in silence.
- Practice doing mindfulness daily: This is not needed for jealousy but you should do it every day.

(Written May 2016 at 14-years-old)

ANGRY DUCKS

Angry ducks hiss and beat nearby ducks. Angry ducks can fight like people. Angry ducks are similar to people.

Angry people have meltdowns. Angry people have arguments. Angry people also hiss. Angry people beat other people and objects.

Here are some ways to stop anger:

- Do Some Exercises: This will cool yourself down when angry. It will also help your body stay healthy and strong.
- Delay your Reaction: This will help you get centered again. Inhale deeply and as you exhale, count to ten or repeat a phrase that helps you relax several times.
- Distract Yourself: Read a good book that will make you feel happy, watch a movie that will make you smile or feel good, and think of a good memory. You

could also try painting, drawing, writing, and more!

- Discuss Your Anger With Someone You Trust: This might make you feel better. It could be a family member, friend, or someone you play or work with. The person you talk to may have experienced it themselves.
- Listen to Music: Listening to music may help you feel better.
- Write To Yourself: I know it might sound silly but it will help you feel a lot lighter once you're done. Write out your anger. Once you have nothing more to say, delete it or tear it up. Use this as a way of letting go of what's bothering you.
- Accept and Know: It's okay to feel angry and be angry.
- Focus: Where do you feel the anger in your body? How does it feel? Does it feel tight or painful? Focus on all of that. Eventually, it should go away. Of course, if it's your first few times it may not work for you because it takes practice.

- Do something: Take a few deep breaths, look at a flower, look at a tree, look at birds, or go for a walk.
- Don't say judgmental things about anger: You'll feel better after you have done this.

I hope you've enjoyed this blog post. See you next time at Emotions With Animals!

(Written May 2016 at 14-years-old)

SAD CATS

Cats yowl and protect themselves by wrapping the tail, crouching low, holding ears in a fearful or cautious manner, and displaying glum whiskers.

People sometimes make noises like cats do when they're sad. People try to protect themselves by forcing the tears into a lump in the throat. People will be silent and thinking.

The people will have a sad smile, half smile, or sad face.

Here's some tips of how not to be sad if you feel like you are sad.

- It's okay to be sad. You don't have to be happy unless you want to get out of the sadness stage.
- Find something that makes you laugh.
- Look at someone who's hilarious to you, smile, read something, watch something, or draw something funny.

(Written April 2016 at 14-years-old)

HAPPY DOGS

Happy dogs like to lick you and smell you. Dogs also like to wag their tail when they like you. The dogs also try to cheer you up too.

People are harder to be happy because they don't accept looking in the current moment instead of the past or future. When they're happy, the people seem more cheerful.

Here's some suggestions on how to be happier:

- Do a grateful exercise: Gratefulness brings the attention away from distress and other opposites of happy. It brings the attention forward to happiness.
- Stop looking for happiness: Realize it is in you already.
- Learn to connect with and accept emotion: Here's how to connect with and accept emotions. Say to yourself repeatedly, I accept emotions. While saying that, ask yourself where you feel

that emotion and focus and breathe in that area.

- Learn And Practice Mindfulness: Going out in nature can help you learn and practice mindfulness. Read "Mindful Goslings" in this book to find more about how you can be mindful.
- Meditation: Meditate every day. If you want, do some intense meditation.
- Otherwise, stick with easy or moderate meditation.

(Written April 2016 at 14-years-old)

MINDFUL GOSLINGS

You have to be calm and very quiet to approach baby geese. If you get loud and perhaps angry, they would just hiss at you or follow you.

If you were meditating, you'd want a quiet and soothing environment around you. If you have any disruptions, you'd explode like a volcano or you'd lose your temper (like hissing and chasing you). Mindfulness is good and very simple.

Here's some ideas that I'd like to share with you:

- Reading: Try reading a calm book for a change.
- Look in nature: Focus on nature.
- Coloring: Coloring will help you keep your mind sharp.
- Here's some ideas from Camilla Downs:
    - Painting
    - Drawing

(Written April 2016 at 14-years-old)

THE LAST COOKIE

THE LAST COOKIE

Once there lived a young fairy princess who was half mermaid, royal human, and flying human. Her name was Mermaidia Princess Fairy-Alia. Mermaidia danced, swam, walked, and flew so good.

One day, she flew to the cookie box and she turned into a princess again when she said, "I am proud to be a fairy, but can you transform me back into a princess."

Suddenly her sister named Bellina flew in and grabbed the final cookie which Mermaidia had wanted so badly. She sat down to think of a solution.

This is the end of part one of the cookie series. What do you think was Mermaidia's solution? What do you think was the flavor of the cookie?

(Written June 2016 at 14-years-old)

COOKIES FOR EVERYONE

Mermaidia had a solution finally and it was to suggest to cut the cookie in half. If you're wondering, the cookie flavor is fruit punch. Mermaidia looked around trying to find Bellina.

Mermaidia found Bellina in the kitchen; preparing to eat the cookie. Finally Mermaidia reached Bellina. Mermaidia said, "I have something to say to you." Bellina asked, "What do you want to say to me, Mermaidia?" So Mermaidia asked Bellina, "Here's what I want to say to you, may I have half of your cookie please?"

That's the end of part two of The Last Cookie. What do you think Bellina said to Mermaidia? Where do you think Mermaidia sat down to think of the solution?

(Written June 2016 at 14-years-old)

BELLINA ANSWERS MERMAIDIA'S QUESTION

Mermaidia had gone to sleep thinking, "When will she give me my answer?" She woke up thinking, "Today is going to be the day when I receive the answer. I can feel it in my bones."

Mermaidia waited so long that she had to flutter, pace, swim, and practice curtsying. Mermaidia sat where she had thought of a solution; which was on a flying chair in the living room.

Finally, Bellina said, "I'm ready to give you my answer." Bellina answered, "Yes, you may have half of the cookie. Thank you for asking, Mermaidia!"

This is the end of part three of The Last Cookie. What do you think Mermaidia and Bellina will do next? How long do you think Mermaidia waited to hear from her sister?

(Written June 2016 at 14-years-old)

WHAT BELLINA AND MERMAIDIA WILL DO NEXT

Mermaidia sat down with Bellina. While Mermaidia and Bellina were each eating their half of a cookie, they began to talk. Here is one of the things Mermaidia said, "I waited 108 hours to find out whether you would say yes."

After they were done talking, they went to bed. When they woke up in the morning, they were very proud. After that, when they wanted a cookie they used the technique that Mermaidia used.

You can use this very technique.

(Written June 2016 at 14-years-old)

APPLE NAMED CALM SPARKLE

Hey, everyone! Are you wondering who is Calm Sparkle? If you answered yes, you've come to the right place. Read on to find out.

Once there lived a small apple whose name was Calamity. The apple didn't know how to say Calamity but she was able to say "Calm Sparkle." So her name was shortened to Calm S.

True to her name, she grew to be a big calm sparkly apple. One day, she didn't seem so calm. She explained, "I'm just anxious to see my relatives. The last time I saw them was when I was a small applet."

So as time went on, she wasn't calm at all. After her relatives left, she admitted she had outgrown her calmness. The apple asked for help and everyone tried to help.

One spring morning, she felt unusually calm. She suddenly realized her calmness had returned. When she announced her calmness had returned, everyone clapped and cheered.

To this day forward, she can be found in everyone's heart. She might be hiding or showing her calmness to your inner self.

(Written June 2016 at 14-years-old)

MISCHIEVOUS POPSICLE

One day, a popsicle named Lemona was causing mischief, but she didn't want any popsicles to see. Apparently, her popsicle friends, Lime-Meringue and Minty Rainbow, thought she was hiding something.

So they asked questions, but she just ignored them. "I want to find out who she's against," said Minty and Lime. Finally they found Licorice Popella in Lemona's ice room. Minty asked if Lemona is against her.

Surprisingly, Licorice responded, "Yes." They wanted to know why Lemona was against her. Lemona wanted to cause mischief on Licorice. So they went to find Lemona to tell her what they'd found out.

Lemona realized her mistake and quickly apologized to Licorice. She was surprised to find that she had been caught. So Lemona explained to Lime and Minty that she wanted to find a red hat to go with her lemon scented dress.

She had thought it would be okay to borrow Licorices' scented hat. So Lemona asked Licorice if she could borrow her hat. Licorice said, "You may use the scented hat. Next time, come to me if you feel mischievous and I'll help you snap out of your mischief!" So

Lemona agreed to come to Licorice if she felt mischievous. From that day forward, you can see Lemona, Minty, Lime, and Licorice hanging out in popsicles you eat. I hope you enjoy my story!

(Written May 2016 at 14-years-old)

JEALOUS CRAYONS

Once upon a time, a crayon named Brick was almost always jealous of his twin Periwinkle Strawberry Star ever since Periwinkle was born. One day, their parents called Indigo and Violet, thought they should find a plan to stop the jealousy.

So they called, asked, walked, explored, and traveled. Finally, they found a crayon named Blueberry Midnight Indigo. The trio crayons headed back to their colorful home. Indigo and Violet called Brick when they got home. Violet pretended to adopt Blueberry. Indigo pretended to tell Brick "Periwinkle has been sent away." Over the next few days, Brick got to know Blueberry. Little did he know, that Indigo and Violet were with Periwinkle who was still in the colorful home. A year passed since Brick had been jealous and Brick had become a great friend (good fake sibling also) to Blueberry.

One day, Violet and Indigo thought it was about time that Brick knew the truth. So Violet and Indigo told Brick the truth and showed Periwinkle who explained she had been in her colorful red and blue room while Indigo and Violet had visited her every day.

So Brick apologized to Periwinkle for being jealous about Periwinkle's name. Periwinkle told her brother that she could change his name to Atomic Brick Red. Brick loved it and from that day forward he was Atomic.

As for Blueberry, he married Periwinkle. Atomic Brick and Blueberry became brothers-in-law. If you look closely, you can hear the new trio laughing, talking, and having fun.

(Written May 2016 at 14-years-old)

ANGRY CANDY

Once upon a time, there lived a red chewy candy who was always angry and her name was Angel. One day, Angel got angry for some unknown reason. Her candy buddies decided to investigate what could have made her angry, but first, they had to look for some possible clues.

While they were investigating, Angel met with her candy friend, Sneaky Spice-Rika who was always acting innocent; but Sneaky was hiding something from Angel. The investigators found strawberry flavored licorice, spices, and mint candy. So they went back to their club called Secret Detective Club to plan their next step of the mystery.

They put together a "talk to" list of suspicious candy suspects with other candy suspects. The candy suspects were Sneaky Spice-Rika, Strawbella, and Sugarlicious.

They set out to talk to Sugarlicious first. "I did see something very unusual, odd, and peculiar this morning." said Sugarlicious, "I saw Sneaky Spice-Rika near Angel".

So the buddies said, "Thank you" and moved on to talk to Strawbella but apparently she didn't see anything strange. Finally, they talked to Sneaky Spice-Rika and she said she was only near Angel to talk to her. So they went to Angel to get more facts and she said it was to comfort her. So the investigators went on to explain the whole story.

When Angel had heard the whole story, she chuckled and explained to them that no one had made her angry but herself. She also said that she had a bad argument with her candy parents, Coca and Choc.

The investigators went back to tell everyone what they had learned. First, they stopped by Sugarlicious to tell her what she had seen was actually an act of kindness. Next, they stopped by Strawbella to tell her that Angel had been angry and she was made angry all on her own.

Lastly, they visited Sneaky Spice-Rika to apologize about suspecting her. The investigators thanked her for being such a great friend. Angel forgot about being angry and never got angry again. If you look closely, you can see Angel in any chewy red candy you or your friends eat.

(Written May 2016 at 14-years-old)

A SAD PRINCESS

Once upon a time, there lived a princess named Liana who cried a lot and almost never stopped. One day when Liana was crying, her parents who were the Queen and King thought they had to do something immediately.

So the Queen and the King thought for several days and nights. Suddenly, they had a fantastic idea and that idea was to make her laugh. So the Queen and King set out on a search to find someone or something to make her laugh out loud.

They found a funny book that would surely make her laugh. So they went home to the castle to see if their theory was right. Surprisingly, the princess laughed and laughed. At first, she was chuckling and the chuckling came bigger.

The Queen and King were relieved. She didn't cry ever again except for joyful tears. If you listen carefully, you might be able to hear her laughing.

*This story was inspired by the movie, *"Barbie and the Diamond Castle"*.

(Written May 2016 at 14-years-old)

A HAPPY FAIRY

Once upon a time, there lived a flower fairy who was almost always happy. Her name was Lilac L. (L. stands for Lily) Jane, like a flower fairy. She was very happy with her life for a long time.

One day while Lilac was fluttering around, she overheard a fairy saying, "Hey, be nice!" and surprisingly Lilac burst into tears. When she calmed down, she decided that she would talk it through with the fairy who had said, "Be nice!" in such a mean voice.

So she set off to find the fairy but the fairy found her first. The fairy said, "I figured you overheard me, so I tried to find you but I couldn't. Anyway, that was my fairy cousin I was talking to. Do you want to be fairy friends?"

Lilac decided the fairy's voice was so calm and kind that she went ahead and said, "Yes."

From that day forward, Lilac could be found with her fairy friend every day at 3:00 p.m.

Of course, she stayed happy and never burst into tears again. If you listen hard, you might be able to hear Lilac and her fairy friend every day at 3:00 p.m.

(Written April 2016 at 14-years-old)

A MINDFUL MERMAID STORY

Once upon a time, there lived a mermaid who always had preferred to be having adventures to staying in her mermaid cave. Her name was Evangeline E. (E stands for Emma) Rose.

One day, her parents wanted her to be like her mermaid siblings. Despite what her parents wanted her to do, she wanted to be full of life. So she went to do some MM (mermaid meditation) to see who was right.

Even the meditation didn't help, so she fretted until a fairy godmother suddenly appeared and Evangeline exclaimed, "Thank goodness! Can you help me decide who's side to take?" So the godmother said, "Oh my goodness! I can help you by telling you to be mindful of your parents' choice."

So Evangeline went to talk over her choice with her parents and after a while, they saw she was very mindful. They could also see that she had a point. So they let her continue to be adventurous and she lived happily ever after. That's the story of how Evangeline learned to be mindful.

If you look carefully, you can see Evangeline being mindful. She might give you mindful advice!

*This story was inspired by the movie, *"The Princess and the Frog"*.

(Written April 2016 at 14-years-old)

FEARFUL SEASONS

Once upon a time, there lived a season named Summerella and she lived fearful, but no other season knew why. On a beautiful day Springel had said, "We can't let this unknown fear pass unknowingly. Let some of our seasons go find the fear."

So the seasons agreed to let some of the seasons go. So they searched high, low, east, and west. Suddenly, just when the seasons were about to give up, they saw something in the distance; but the seasons couldn't fly. So, they set off to find something on which to ride.

Finally they found something to ride but the fear was getting away. So they sped up and eventually they caught up to the fear. The fear was a season animal who had run away. So they rounded up the season animal and brought it back to Springel.

The seasons asked Springel what they should do with the season animal that ran away. Springel suggested they keep it with the other secured season animals. After they were done, they went to tell Summerella her fear was gone.

To this day forward, you can find Summerella in Summer, Springel in Spring, Winterfell in Winter, and Autumn-Stella in Autumn. I hope you enjoyed!

(Written June 2016 at 14-years-old)

GRACEFUL PLANETS

Once upon a time, there lived a planet named Blue Moon who had always wanted to be graceful, but her parental planets didn't agree yet. She needed proof to prove she wanted to be graceful but she didn't know yet what proof.

She went to Wild Fruit planet who was very wise. Wild told her to be patient. So she was patient but one day the idea goes into her circular head. She set out to find a graceful planetary animal who would be given to her parental planets as proof.

Finally, after looking several planetary nights and days, she found a planet animal called Nebula Sparkles. The animal was incredibly graceful and she asked the animal if she wanted to go back with her to Planetary Moon Sky.

The animal said, "Yes, you may take me back to Moon Sky". When they arrived, she was greeted by her parental planets and she gave them the animal. Blue Moon explained that she got the animal for her proof that she was graceful.

Her parental planets talked it over. They finally agreed that she could be graceful. So now whenever you see the Blue Moon, just remember this legend and you may see her parental planets in the distance.

(Written May 2016 at 14-years-old)

LEGENDS, TALES, AND ADVENTURES

MANDALA LEGEND

Once upon a time, there lived a mandala who lived alone. One day, the mandala went for a walk. The mandala came along a little hole with golden light shining through. The mandala thought, "What is that golden light?"

So the mandala decided to take a peek. The mandala was very surprised that inside the hole was another mandala living alone. Furthermore, that mandala used sunlight to help bring peace to his home.

She noticed the other mandala looking around the small room and exclaimed, "Goodness me,

I didn't see anyone peeking through the sunlight." Even so, she invited the mandala in and she noticed the mandala enjoying the sunlight as well. So if you ever see a mandala in the sunlight, that could have been a distant relative of the mandala.

(Written June 2017 at 15-years-old)

A CHRISTMAS STORY

Once there was a Christmas angel named Holly. Holly wanted to find a way to make Christmas more memorable than ever. So Holly set out to do some research. She found that the only way to do that was to put a sprig of holly in doorways.

After Holly spruced some holly, she went to her friend Mistletoe. Holly told her about her idea and Mistletoe suggested that she transform holly into mistletoe. Mistletoe said that she'd help with the mistletoe. Holly came up with another idea and she said, "Let's wait until Christmas Eve to do it."

Holly told Mistletoe the plan. The plan was for Mistletoe to stand behind Holly and when Holly gave the signal Mistletoe would change the holly to mistletoe. Mistletoe agreed to the plan. On Christmas Eve, Holly and Mistletoe tested their magic.

After they tested their magic, they announced that Christmas would never again be the same. Mistletoe and Holly prepared for the trick fast. By the time they were prepared, everyone was there.

So Mistletoe was standing behind Holly. Holly aimed her hand toward the holly. Holly gave the secret signal to Mistletoe. When Mistletoe got the signal, she immediately transformed all the hollies into mistletoe.

The people who watched clapped in amazement. Little did they know, the mistletoe and holly were magical. The people went back to their Christmas celebration. The Christmas spirit was stronger than before.

To this day, you can feel the Christmas spirit presence.

(Written January 2017 at 15-years-old)

THE GREAT UNIVERSE

It all started on a warm summer night in a cozy home where a girl lay sleeping, until she felt a jolt and she realized she wasn't in her home anymore. She thought, "Why is there nothing?" and she got her answer. An echoing voice said, "You are where the universe began. It's up to you to make the planets including Earth. Once you've made Earth, start creating. Have fun!"

So the girl quickly discovered she could use her mind and creativity to make everything. First, she designed Earth to look sparkly, clean, and rainbow colored. Second, she made other planets look like the colors of the rainbow. She went into Earth and saw she needed to make the moon and stars. So she made the moon look and taste like cheese. She made stars look like glitter.

She made the sky look indigo when it was daytime. She exited Earth to put the blue colored sun near Earth. She entered Earth again and realized she needed to plant some plants. Luckily, she had some seeds in her pocket. She planted them. She added orange water to Earth to help the plants. She also needed rain. So she made red rain by circling her hand. She made green clouds too.

She realized she was lonely so she added animals of different colors. She created yellow grass so she could rest. Soon the animals became bored with just the little girl. The animals spoke to the girl about being lonely. She said, "No problem. I can make humans; but first, I need to set aside some land for roads, buildings, homes, shops, stores, and more."

As she spoke, she created all the other things humans needed. After that, she formed the first two people. She also cast a spell to make a child, and to make it grow. The humans were magenta. The animals were amazed at how quickly the humans formed and adapted.

She thought she was done, but the voice spoke to her saying that she would have to use creativity, quick thinking, and more. So she tried casting a spell to make the years speed by but it didn't go as planned.

She made a makeshift bed and tried to get into her cozy home. That didn't work so she tried to get the people and animals to help her. They saw a note on the palm tree. The girl was able to reach it. She realized it was a riddle. She realized all she had do was fall asleep.

Before she fell asleep, she cast one final spell and it was the days of the week, months, and years. She fell asleep after that. There was a surprising jolt and she woke up. She was happy to find herself back in her bedroom. She couldn't help thinking it was all a dream.

Just then, a friendly voice explained that it wasn't a dream. It was morning.

She went to the kitchen to tell her parents the most amazing thing happened to her. Her parents explained to her she had a real vision.

Years later, she grew up to become a beloved author. Her name was Morgana and she had been eleven-years-old when the amazing thing happened. She lived in Australia at the time. She loved the book *"Anne of Green Gables."* She thought it described her life perfectly.

The End!

*This story was inspired by the movie, *"The Little Mermaid"*.

(Written September 2016 at 15-years-old)

A HALLOWEEN STORY

Once upon a Halloween, there lived a fairy and her princess who enjoyed Halloween every year. One Halloween, the fairy asked, "Are you going as a fairy? If you are, I could give you some hints. I am going as a princess. I want some hints from you, please."

"Yes, I'm dressing as a fairy. I need some fairy tips from you, please. Wow, I could give you princess tips and hints," said the princess. The princess and the fairy are going to a Halloween party and they are going as a fairy and princess. They give professional tips and hints every year to each other.

"You did a magnificent job. The makeup is fantastic. Does my makeup look ok?" said the princess. "Yes, you did a splendid job. Thank you." Once they were at the Halloween costume party, they had fun and got plenty of candy from trick treating.

When they got home, they were so tired that they collapsed into bed after they took off their costumes. They had scary, fun, and silly Halloween dreams.

Happy Halloween!

(Written October 2016 at 15-years-old)

A HAPPY WORLD

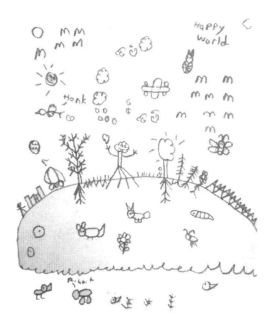

I just got inspired by a drawing I drew. Here's a story based on the drawing.

One day, a bird picked up a seed to eat. A few minutes later, the bird decided that it wasn't the right seed. The bird threw it back down. That was the beginning of the Happy World.

As the years past, the tree grew until it had several branches and a strong trunk. The strong tree became known as the Happy Tree. The Happy Tree decided to produce a seed. The seed grew with happiness and love. One day, the seed blossomed into a young beautiful tree that didn't grow much after that point.

The young tree became known as the Amazing Beauty Tree. The Amazing Beauty Tree saw the Happy Tree. Suddenly, she realized that she wanted to know who produced her. She asked the Happy Tree if it was him who planted her. He said, "Yes," and Amazing Beauty wanted to produce a seed of her own.

She let the bird fly the seed to the Happy World. The seed became a thin beautiful conifer tree. The tree produced identical seeds until there was almost no room to plant seeds. After that the trees started planting grass seeds. After the grass had grown, there was no room to plant seeds.

A few years later, the several earthquakes that would become the mountains shook the world. The trees, birds, and grass survived. They noticed something different about the landscape and they saw triangular tall figures. They soon realized that they had seen a mountain. About the same time, their roots filled with water and animals.

One year later, humans discovered the Happy World and decided to make a small town out of it. They also made cars, rockets, and kites. The sun, clouds, rain, hail, snow, and thunderstorms were always there but they were nicer than outside of the Happy World. Everyone lived happily.

If you go into a forest, you will realize that the Happy World is the forest.

(Written July 2016 at 14-years-old)

REACH FOR THE STARS

This includes two stories, one non-fiction inspiration, and a fiction interview. Let's start with the non-fiction story.

One day, my body decided I was ready to try the ladder at my therapy place. Slowly but surely, my body had decided to try the stairs. Now I can easily walk up them alone without being scared. Ever since, I've been proud to have touched the stars. If anyone wonders what's next, it's escalators.

Let's move on to the fantasy version of a story. I hope you enjoyed the first story!

Once, a young girl named Rainbow had wanted to be able to go down stairs for a long time but her body wasn't ready to do it. Many years past before her body started to sense that she wanted to achieve the goal. When she was probably fourteen, her body was able to take the hint fully. So she took her time up until Wednesday when she achieved the goal. She was very excited. She was reaching toward the stars.

Let's move on to the interview. This is where you will find more details about the first story. Speaking of story, I hope you enjoyed the second story. (If you are wondering, this writing is inspiration based).

Rainbow: Hey, Lillian! Are you ready to start the interview? I'm definitely ready to start.

Lillian: Hey, Rainbow! Yes, I'm ready. It's awesome that you're ready to start.

Rainbow: How did you originally start?

Lillian: Good question! I started by using a step stool for kids.

Rainbow: Wow. What was your progression steps?

Lillian: My order was step stool, ladder, and stairs. Anything else you would like to know?

Rainbow: No, I don't think so. Let's end it here. Bye, nice meeting you!

Lillian: Bye, Rainbow!

(Written July 2016 at 14-years-old)

MELODY THE DOG

You're about to enter a funny interview with Melody the Dog.

Annie: Hey there! Are you ready to do some digging?

Melody: Hey! Yes. I'm ready to start digging!

Annie: Great! Do you have pups?

Melody: Yes, I have ten puppies. Thanks for asking that question!

Annie: You're welcome! What are the puppies' names?

Melody: Buster, Digger, Finder, Seeker, Princess, Emily, Bubbles, Peaches, Lily, and Stefanie are the names of the puppies. Do you have puppies?

Annie: I'm human and I have children. Who are you married to?

Melody: I'm married to King the 2nd. Are you married also?

Annie: Yes, I'm married. What's your life like being a dog?

Melody: We dig, find things, seek stuff, and bust things; but we have a certain time for everything. Do you have a certain time for everything?

Annie: Yes, I do. What is your schedule?

Melody: My schedule is to wake up at 5:00 a.m., get some food for breakfast, wake up the kids, have fun, lunch, have more fun, dinner, and go to bed. Do you have any other questions?

Annie: Wow! Yes, I do.

Melody: OK. I am willing to answer your questions.

Annie: I'm excited for Halloween! Are you excited?

Melody: Yes. Do you think we should wrap up our conversation?

Annie: Yes, I think we should. Farewell, it was nice talking to you.

Melody: OK, it was a nice pleasure to meet you. See you soon, Annie.

Annie and Melody: This is the end of the Q&A!

*This interview was inspired by the movie, *"The Little Mermaid 2"*.

(Written May 2016 at 14-years-old)

SAPHIRE AND TOPAZ MYSTERY SOLVER

Relax and take a deep breath. You are about to enter a gemstone's mystery.

Once upon a time, there lived two detectives who were named Sapphire and Topaz. They had already solved three mysteries. This is their fourth mystery together.

One day, they were walking when they suddenly saw a mystery. They suspected that someone or something was following them. They went home to get an idea of what it could be.

Then they went back to the scene with a magnificent idea to try out. The magnificent idea was to get some yummy food at a local gem restaurant and use it to catch the someone or something.

First, they got some food along the way too because they were hungry. They walked back to the scene after that. Secondly, they put the food on the sidewalk and looked for a nearby hidden spot to wait.

Fortunately, they saw a bush and a tree; and they hid in those places. Shortly after, they saw a gem animal they'd never seen before. So they went to investigate but the gem animal noticed them looking at her.

The gem animal laughed and said, "Hello there! I'm Gem-Topia and I am your new gem neighbor. Can you tell me who both of you are?"

"Hey there! Nice to meet you, Gem-Topia. I am Sapphire and this is Topaz," said Sapphire with a chuckle. So the trio became friends. They spent time together and they were inseparable. I hope you enjoyed my story!

(Written May 2016 at 14-years-old)

THE ADVENTUROUS PINEAPPLE FAMILY

Be aware, it might make you very hungry and have a craving for pineapple.

Once upon a time, there lived a pineapple family who were always adventurous. The pineapple family explored Paprika and they visited a spice called Pepper who suggested they visit Applicious and so they did.

In Applicious, they met a fruit named Candy-Apple and she had asked if they'd visited Melon Land. The pineapple family said that they hadn't visited.

So they visited Melon Land. There they met a melon called Honey Water and she suggested Fruit Land. Apparently, they hadn't explored Fruit Land.

In Fruit Land, they saw pineapples, apples, candy fruit, melons, and other fruit. The pineapple wanted to settle down but they wanted to check out Candy Land and Chip Land suggested by Peachy Orange.

So the pineapple family set off for Candy Land and they happened to eat candied pineapple. They met Candied Apple and her Candy Fruit friends. They headed to Chip Land next. While there, they ate pineapple chips. The family met cheddar and her chip friends.

The family went back to Pineapple Land to pack their possessions and head back to Fruit Land. The pineapple family was still adventurous but they stayed close to Fruit Land.

I hope you enjoyed my pineapple story!

(Written May 2016 at 14-years-old)

A CAT WITH MAGIC POWERS

Take a deep breath and enter the magical cat story below.

Once upon a time, there was a cat named Maggie McRita who wanted to be different from every other cat. So she went to her cat books and read but couldn't get any ideas.

After she finished reading, she decided to research on her cat laptop. She discovered so many ideas and she brainstormed to choose the best idea yet. The best idea was to learn some magic and become famous. She set out for her kitten books again; which were in the cat fun room.

This time she read magic cat books; and she looked at the beginner tricks. She assumed that all the magic was going to be slightly easier than her kitten chores.

She decided to do a coin trick as her first trick. She decided to do a card trick as her next magic trick at 6:00 p.m. PST or 9:00 p.m EST.

She practiced until bedtime and she got so good. She had a good idea. She had started to perform in front of her whole cat family.

She started performing for other cats who lived in the country and they started asking her to perform at cat birthday parties. She started getting famous doing her magic tricks.

She wanted a lot of cats to help out too and she wanted a mate. Soon, she was traveling to places she had always dreamed of going.

She finally found a cat who wanted to mate with her and his name was Concertino. She fell in love but she kept on doing her magic tricks and they both had the same clever idea.

She got married to Concertino three months later. She and Concertino did magic tricks and traveled together to places they always dreamed of going.

They had two twin kittens named Water and Earth. As the kittens grew, they helped with magic but they really wanted to be artists. When they were old enough, they told the truth. Maggie wasn't disappointed in them, she figured that was what they were up to.

So, off they went and they both found mates that were also twins. They offered to be in just one house. So they lived in a cat mansion. The mates wanted to become artists also. So, Water and Earth set off to teach their mates as much as they knew.

Shortly afterward, they each had four babies. Meanwhile, Maggie had some health issues and she was unable to do magic during that time. So the rest of the family helped her to do magic until she was healthy again. She went onward to doing challenging tricks.

One day while Maggie was practicing, she fell on her paw weirdly. The paw hurt so much that it was bleeding and she couldn't get up. So the rest of the family went to look for the cat doctor. They found the cat doctor and the family told her that Maggie had hurt her ankle and to come as fast as she can.

After a few seconds, the doctor arrived. The doctor told the family, including Maggie, that she had a broken ankle and she had to sit in a wheelchair for a few days. Shortly afterward, she began to walk on crutches for a month. After the month had passed, she walked with a glittery rainbow walker for the rest of the year.

After the last of the year had past, she was able to walk again. She was advised not to do any advanced magic tricks that involved her paws. She kept that warning for years to come and when her health fell for the last time, no one was able to help her at all. She slipped into a coma that lasted a few weeks; and the coma kept coming back after a few weeks more.

Then the coma kept getting worse until she slept the whole time. Eventually, her breathing slowed down until it was nothing at all. At that point, her death had struck her almost immediately and they thought that she was just holding her breath. Her whole family was completely devastated and that was only her second life. They no longer did magic.

However, they remembered her for the rest of their lives. They put her in the cat Hall of

Famous Cats. Every cat who didn't know her asked to learn about her from someone who knew her.

The End

(Written September 2015 at 13-years-old)

WHERE WOULD YOU FLY

You are about to enter a writing and inspiring world. So hang onto your memories on Earth! Look below and you'll see the writing prompt and story.

If you were a bird and you could fly anywhere, where would you go?

If I were a bird and I could fly anywhere, I would go to a tropical island where I could have all that's needed. Look below for my story.

A Bird Flies Over An Island

I lived happily with my owner until one day; I was looking for my owner when I saw something below. I flew down to investigate and explore. I had found this was the island of the Colorful Fairies. When I saw the Fairies, I asked them where my owner was and found out that my owner had went to heaven.

The Fairies said my real family was here. So I set out to find them. I asked around and I was about to give up when a fruit fairy asked, "Is that your family." I told her, "Yes!"

My family asked me what happened to my owner. So I told them, he went to heaven. They felt sorry for me. They said that I was welcome to stay with them as long as I didn't grab food before the rest of my family did.

I stayed as long as I could. I knew that I had to return to Hawaii. I had to be in a pet store again; but this time, nobody came. So I mated and had six baby birds; but, I never forgot my family.

Five years later, I decided to visit the island with my new parts of family. They loved to see their grand-birds and my mate. I promised I'd come back every two years until they went up to heaven and all went well.

The End

(Written August 2015 at 13-years-old)

LIFE AS AN AUTUMN GOLD APPLE

You are about to enter a life of an apple that you might know about.

I was born as a seed in November 19, 1900. Until spring arrived, I slept. When I woke up, I was a tree. I grew apples and people came and picked the apples off of me. Then the people made new seeds. After my apples were gone, everyone sat under me.

I felt loved until autumn. The leaves started falling off me for the kids to play with.

Finally, winter came and I fell asleep. When I woke up again, I had apple blossoms on me. Then, I grew more apples.

Meanwhile, the seeds from my apples were young trees and they did the same thing. As I got older, more people were able to play on me. One day, I got so old no one was able to play with me. That night, a strong thunderstorm tore one of my branches.

So they had to cut me down. They had a funeral for me. I was forty-nine years old. From then on, the people used my stump as something useful. The other trees lived to be 100-years-old.

To this day, my apples are all over the world. So whenever you eat an autumn gold apple, just remember this story.

(Written June 2015 at 13-years-old)

A REALISTIC WORLD BEYOND YOUR EYES

Hi there, everyone! Please note that the words are in English. You're about to enter a realistic world that will pull you inside the realistic world which is called Cinnamon Extraordinary Planet.

"Mother, where are my cinnamon scented dresses?" asked a 10-cinnamon-cakes-old girl (which is 15-years-old in earth years). "Campari, sorry but I just put them in a wet donut roll (a washer) and they won't be done until it's dry," answered Mother as she applied lipstick on her lips. "Oh fine, do I have to wear cinnamon shirts?" asked Campari as she pouted around the cinnamon room.

"Oh, hi there! I didn't see you come in! My name is Campari. My mother mentioned it earlier. My mother's name is Sweet Cinnamon Dazzle although she likes going by SCD or Mother. I have a father who works at a cinnamon factory and I hardly see him but I do know his name which is Twisty Spice Herb and

he also likes to go by TSH or Father. My best friend is Splendid Apple Cinnamon. She likes going by her full name," explained Campari Dazzle as she looked at her mother with a cinnamon look.

"So, you must be a world visitor. Campari told me about you. Nice to meet you!" said Mother as she looked at the reader. "Campari has a cinnamon dance tonight and is very excited to be going there," said Mother in a joking way.

So Campari got ready for the dance and she saw Sherbet waiting for her so she said "Goodbye, Mother!" so fast that her mother didn't get to tell her to have fun. The dancing partners headed to the dance.

When they got there, they danced until midnight to get some cinnamon rolls. After that, they danced some more. They danced out onto the cinnamon scented balcony in the moonlight and kissed briefly. Shortly after that, they went inside and left the dance.

"Mother, I had the most wonderful time at the dance." said Campari dreamily. "Well, that's great!" said Mother. Then they both went to sleep.

The next morning, Campari said "I'm in love," and her mother said "Who are you in love with?" and she responded "Sherbet." "Do you want to get married yet?" said Mother. "Mother, I want to have dates with him first," said Campari.

So the couple set out on several dates a few days later. Just a month after, Sherbet asked "Will you marry me, my cinnamon bun?" and of course she couldn't say no, so she said "Yes, I'll marry you!" Then they went out to find Campari's mother.

"Oh, Campari! You must be Sherbet! You came to tell me you want a wedding". Shortly after that, the wedding begins and all Sherbet and Campari's families and friends came.

And they lived happily ever after.

(Written May 2015 at 13-years-old)

A FRIENDSHIP BETWEEN FOUR TYPES OF CANDY

You are about to enter a story about four candies and their friendship; with a moral.

Jellybean went walking and found his friend Rocky (also known as Rock Candy). So Jellybean told him his wish of how he wanted to be seen. After that, Rocky set off to help his friend with a flyer. Shortly after, he ran into Orange Slice.

Campari Dazzle

Spendid Apple Cinnamon

So he told Orange all about it. Before long, Orange set off to help Jellybean. After that, the candies became desperate and determined to help Jellybean.

A few days later, they ran into Jellybean and they told him their plan and he liked it. The plan was to let Jellybean do funny tricks. In two days, they put on a show.

In just two months, he got extremely popular. He was happy that his wish came true. From that day, they became best friends.

The moral of that story was if you wish something badly and you tell someone; chances are you might just get your wish.

(Written June 2015 at 13-years-old)

FRUIT FASHION

One day a strawberry named Juicy Fashion was walking and said "Perfect day for fashion". She accidentally bumped into a blueberry named Tamed Blueberry at the moment. He said

"What a fantastic idea". So they sent out invitations.

Orange said she'd come. So did all the other fruits. All the males had to be judges, audience, and attendants; while females could be in the fashion show. You'll never guess who won the fashion show!

Did I hear you say Juicy Fashion? Well you're correct! She got a large trophy and a piece of fruit cake. Everyone congratulated her!

The End.

(Written July 2014 at 12-years-old)

149

THE SECRET PLACE

My family went to a funeral for my Aunt Cassandra in Savannah, Georgia. The funeral had quiet talking, weeping, and posters. My family hung posters of my Aunt Cassie on the wall; though we kept some so we could remember her.

My name is Rose Safety Topple; although my friends just call me Rose. Get to know more people in my family: My cousin, Jewel; my father, John; my mother-in-law, Samantha; my step-mother, Tanya; my grandmother, Sarah; my mother, Sasha; my grandfather, Alex; and my nephew, Joey. This story is mostly about me and my mother, Sasha.

My Uncle Al (which is short for Allie) pushed over to me a sparkly, smooth, blue bag and the bag was also shiny too. "This was your Aunt's favorite childhood bag when she was your age," said Uncle Al. Two days later I opened the bag and here's what I saw inside the bag:

An old letter perfumed to make it smell like roses.

When I put books in the bag, every time they disappeared. I didn't know what was the magic in the bag so I just referred to it as, "The Secret Place". Later I inherited Morse Code and a few minutes later, the bag grabbed me. I suddenly realized it was The Secret Place to where the books were taken. This was my Aunt Cassie's beloved place that she left for me to explore and learn. Her world was the Famous World.

I had wondered where the books had gone. Later, I found out that it was a time traveling rotation. When it was time to leave, a traveling bald eagle ate me as if I were a worm and I ended up in Hawaii.

In estimation, it took five months to get back. I got stuck at the airport so I had to call my mother, Sasha. She questioned how I ended up in the airport.

When I finally got back to our home in Reno, Nevada, the bag had shrunk. Ever since then I never used it again; not even for books. Today

I've made the decision to call the bag, "Magic Bag."

Here are some reasons why: The bag had spoke to me once or twice. Another time it turned into animals like a whale or fish. It even turned into a human and it told me I was hurting its feelings. I sent it instantly to the post office and it has traveled around the world since then. Who knows? You might even have kept the bag for your own.

If you own it, I'm pretty sure that the magic wore out. I learned my lesson those days. Now that I'm grown up, I always save those kinds of memories.

If you can't tell if it's my bag, ask someone for the details of the bag. If you see a "lost" sign, it just might have been my bag. Who cares if it's dusty, old looking, odd shaped, and dirty too! I might clean it up, perhaps.

(Written May 2014 at 12-years-old)

ALSATIAN AND HIS FAMILY – AN ALL LANGUAGE LEGEND

Way back in 1019, there was a man who had such a talent that nobody could resist; which was writing science books. That's a different story though.

His name is Alsatian Samaria. He was born in Dream City at 12:03 p.m. in 1200 B.C. He met Artful in 1299 at Gold Valley City. Then in 1890 he got married to Artful.

In 1894 they had eighteen children. A few of them are Sally, Jetson, and Glees. When Alsatian's wife Artful died he changed his name to Al and when Al died he became Alaska which is the 49th today.

To this day he remains Alaska who borders Hawaii.

(Written February 2014 at 12-years-old)

TRUTHFUL ART – A CHINESE LEGEND

Way back in the 1920s there was a lady in her mid-twenties who thought, "The art I have in my mind will eventually happen soon." Her name was Artful. Three days later she created three paintings named Liletta, Tinletta, and Ciletta.

When Artful wasn't around the three paintings talked about for whom they were thought to be made. One day Artful thought she had heard the three paintings talk, but she thinks that she heard nothing.

After that day, she hid behind a door and listened. Then she walked in and asked them about what they were talking. So they lied then. Artful had thought, "What can I do to make them truthful paintings?"

Just then a magical creature had appeared and it told Artful to take as many wishes as she could take. So three seconds later, they told the truth to Artful who explained the whole thing to them.

Artful was so pleased that she entered all three of the paintings in an art contest. Five days later, they won first prize and Artful was amazed.

To this day, they can be seen in art museums or an art book.

(Written February 2014 at 13-years-old)

THE MYTH OF THE UNUSUAL RAINBOW DECADES

Once upon a decade it was the year 1600 when the most unusual thing happened. The decade was known as Rainbow Sky.

Everything wasn't color yet. Suddenly, everything was in a rainbow. I happened to look up that night and saw that there was a beautiful rainbow moon. Then I looked down and saw that my shoes were rainbow colored. I was so surprised that I sat down and watched the news.

"Someone seems to think that there was a flash of invisible light," says the news person. "Seems to me that it will be a decade before the colorful world is gone," he added.

Young and Old

I didn't know what a decade was so I happened to ask. My mother explained that a decade was when it'd be 1700. I also asked my mother, Sunny B. Snowy, if I would be alive then. But she said, "No, you won't be alive."

As days went by, my eyes were beginning to adjust. By the way, I'm Augustine Blue Snowy. Finally, it's year 1620. I'm an adult now.

I am still thinking about what my mother had said to me twenty years ago. I am nearing the end of life. I have three girls. It's 1630 now and I'm sick with a bad disease.

Death and Disappearance

Augustine has passed away. The date is August 1630. I'm Sephia, one of Augustine's girls.

Many years later, the grown-up girls are sitting reading the news. They found out that the rainbow decade was over. But when they looked outside and saw that the sky was light blue and everything was colored like it is today. Who knows when it will turn black and white again!

Black and White Returns to the World

The women hadn't seen anything like it; as Augustine hadn't seen anything like the rainbow decade. But eventually as the years went on, the women were finally able to manage the black and white.

When the rainbow decade came back, then the colored world came back. It went on like this until 1919. The women exclaimed, "It seems like Mother Nature had a fight with color."

So, Mother Nature decided to keep the colored world.

(Written 2013 at 12-years-old)

WITCH CREATION

Once upon a Halloween, a witch was born on October 31,1899 and she had a pet named Angelic.

When she grew up, she had a witch-daughter that was born on October 30, 2013. Her name was Marcia Angel-weather. When the witch's daughter was 19-years-old, the witch learned that she had weather magic instead of Halloween magic that scares people from her clever daughter Marcia.

So Ms. Angel put an alarm on her rose so she knew when to change the weather. She's still out there changing weather and she can be seen in the clouds. They all lived happily ever after.

*This story was inspired by the movie, *"Sleeping Beauty"*.

(Written October 2013 at 12-years-old)

PATTY'S LOVE AND LILLIAN'S STYLE, CAMILLA'S FUN, THOMAS' COOLNESS, AND FRANK'S FUNNINESS

Once upon a time there was someone named Patty's Love. She was sweet, but one day she became sick and The Romanos could not be kind and gentle without her.

Plus, one day the Romanos chimed the butterfly chimes, then came up with an idea. So they made her lunch and Patty's Love was better.

(Written 2011 at 10-years-old)

THE STORM IS COMING

Oh! It is rain!
Oh! Frank! There's a storm coming
There's a cat up the tree.

Oh! Know.
The storm stopped.
But was a little bit of storm left.

Oh! The justred. Storm is gone now!
Hooray! Hooray! Hooray!
They are having the party now!

The End!

(Written June 2008 at 6-years-old)

THE BEAR EATS BEES

Once upon,
there was
a bear;
had
to
eat
the bees.
And rrrr!
And he did!
The end!

(Written May 2008 at 6-years-old)

THE WHALE WHO WORE CLOTHES

There once was a whale who wore clothes. Her name was Herrit Sneardough and she lived in a house in the Wooden Ocean. Her favorite shirt was yellow with the words "Sun Kissed" printed on it. She liked to wear it with a green flowered skirt.

Every morning when she woke up she gave her little brother, Bleazet Sneardough, a kiss on the cheek. Then she ate breakfast. After breakfast, Herrit went to school at Loresting Elementary. She was in the first grade in Mrs. Rose's class.

At school, Herrit played with the other ocean children in her class. She also read books and drew pictures. Herrit was learning how to write the letters of the alphabet. Herrit's mom and little brother, Bleazit, picked her up from school at 3:15 p.m. When they got home they played with cars, fire trucks, airplanes, boats, and buses.

Next, Herrit did her homework. She had to read two books. Herrit really liked to read. She also had to do math homework. Herrit was learning how to tell time and all about clocks. Not too long after she was done with homework it was time for dinner. Herrit got to have a small donut and a cookie for dessert.

Before bedtime Herrit read books. Then her mom and dad read her a book. Bleazit went to bed before Herrit because he was only two years old.

Herrit turned on her favorite music and her mom tucked her into bed. Then Herrit and her mom talked about Herrit's Happy Thoughts for the day. These thoughts helped her to fall asleep and have sweet dreams. She fell asleep in five minutes and dreamed about her school friend, Lillian.

And that is all about Herrit Sneardough's day. So if you are ever in the Wooden Ocean, come by and visit the Sneardoughs.

*Written with help from Camilla Downs.

(Written August 7 2007 at 5-years-old)

NEVER SLEEP WITH BEARS

You should never sleep with bears because
your feet might get squished.

You should never sleep with bears because you
might lose your hat.

You should never sleep with bears because
your cat might get out.

You should never sleep with bears because
your hair might get pulled.

You should never sleep with bears because
your stomach might get poked.

You should never sleep with bears because you
might get dirt in your eyes.

You should never sleep with bears because you
might get cramps in your legs.

You should never sleep with bears because it might smell really bad and make you sneeze.

You should never sleep with bears because it might be really loud and hurt your ears.

You should never sleep with bears because it might get really hot.

You should never sleep with bears because you have to be very quiet and that's no fun.

You should never sleep with bears because the bears might hurt your cheek when they give you a goodnight kiss.

Maybe you should sleep with a small fluffy teddy bear instead!

The End!

*Written with help from Camilla Downs

(Written January 2007 at 5-years-old)

THE CAT WHO WORE GLASSES – THE MYSTERY OF THE MISSING FRIEND

Once upon a time there was an old brown cat named Thomas who wore glasses. He lived in a stone house in Darwin, Australia with his momma, daddy, his friend, Lillian, and a dog with brown spots named Lucy.

Every morning Thomas and Lillian each took one vitamin. Then they ate strawberry waffles with an apple and drank water. Thomas also had a glass of milk. If they ate all of their breakfast, they each got a vanilla cookie.

But, on this morning, Thomas could not find his friend Lillian anywhere.

He looked in Lillian's bed. She was not there.

He looked in the office and guest bedroom. She was not there.

He looked in the bathroom. She was not there. He looked in the basement and in the closets. She was not there.

He looked in the stove and on the roof. She was not there.

He looked in the backyard and the front yard. She was not there.

He looked in the garage and the workshop. She was not there.

Thomas was beginning to get worried. So, he began to daydream about where Lillian was and what she might be doing.

Was she eating fresh, warm, chocolate chip cookies at Joe's Bakery? Thomas phoned Joe to see if she was there. She was not.

Maybe she was sleeping at her Fishing Grandma and Fishing Grandpa's house. Thomas called them to ask if Lillian was there. She was not.

Maybe she was seeing Dr. Bob, the dentist, for a cleaning. He called Dr. Bob's office. She was not there.

Was she blowing bubbles at the park, Thomas wondered.

Maybe she was flying in an airplane in the big, beautiful sky. He went outside to look in the sky. She was not there.

Maybe she was at the science museum. Thomas called the museum. She was not there.

Maybe she was eating macaroni and cheese and a banana at the HeyNo Restaurant. He called the HeyNo. She was not there.

Maybe she was …… Thomas heard a noise in the garage. Then he heard the door open and close. He thought he heard Lillian laughing and clapping.

He did! Lillian came around the corner and said, "Hi Thomas." Thomas stomped his foot and asked where she had been. Don't be silly Thomas. "I have been at the zoo with my daddy," said Lillian.

She told Thomas that she had eaten an apple, sour candy, and a peanut butter cookie. And, not to worry because she ate her vitamin at the zoo.

Lillian explained that she saw ten elephants with really long trunks and they had their mouths open, too. She played on the elephants trunks. They lifted her high above their heads. Then, she pinched one of the elephants on his cheek and he cried. She didn't mean to hurt him. So she told him she was very sorry and she bought him a bag of peanuts to make him feel better.

Which reminded Lillian that she had brought Thomas cotton candy from the zoo. Thomas was so happy his friend Lillian was home and that she brought him cotton candy.

Thomas was relieved that the mystery of the missing friend had been solved. As he drifted to sleep that night, he wondered what mystery would happen next.

The End!

*Written with help from Camilla Downs.

(Written August 2006 at 4-years-old)

FUN ON THE FARM

There once was a farm in Animalia. A little girl named Lillian lived on the farm with her mom, dad, and little brother. But this story is not about them.

This story is about all the animals that lived on the farm. Cows, sheep, horses, mice, rabbits, cats, dogs, ducks, pigs, and chickens lived on the farm, too. Let's spend a day with these animals and you can decide if they really have fun on the farm.

Three cows had milk to drink and then went to sleep in the garden. Then the cows played Bingo with ten little girls. Next the cows wore red hats and clapped.

Eleven sheep slept on hay upstairs in the barn. Then the sheep read ten books about sleeping. Next, the eleven sheep ate cereal and ten cookies in Lillian's room.

Twenty two horses slept in the flower garden. Then the horses took turns on the swing. Next, the horses clapped and played with straw hats.

Eleven mice were sleeping on hay in the barn. Then, the mice played dominoes with three cats. Next, the eleven mice climbed a tree and each ate one cherry.

Four rabbits ate carrots in the garden. Then, the rabbits went to sleep upstairs in the barn with Lillian's mom. Next, the four rabbits went outside and slid on the slide with Lillian's mom.

Thirty three cats put beads in storage bags with forty four dogs. Then, the cats went to sleep on the sofa. Next, the thirty three cats each ate one apple, one waffle, and a bowl of cereal at Lillian's table in the guest bedroom.

Twenty two dogs slept on the floor upstairs with Lillian's mom in her bedroom. Then, the dogs each ate one cherry in the cherry tree. Next, the twenty two dogs played dominoes in the guest bedroom.

Forty four ducks slurped water from the bathroom sink. Then the ducks played cards with the letter "I". Next, the forty four ducks went to sleep upstairs with Lillian's mom in her bed.

Ten pigs played hide-n-seek with twenty two mice in the field. Then the ten pigs read seven books about elephants and went to sleep in the barn. Next, the ten pigs wore hats and each ate one cookie, a bowl of cereal, cheese toast, and chips with apple juice.

Forty four chickens slept on the bed in the guest bedroom. Then the chickens wore slippers and played dominoes. Next, the forty four chickens thread beads and made necklaces and bracelets.

Now. Don't you think those silly animals have fun on the farm?

The End!

*Written with help from Camilla Downs

(Written June 2006 at 4-years-old)

AMAZING NATURE PARTY

THE FANTASTIC IDEA

One day, a nature group was doing great with their nature learning. They thought they should have a theme party. Can you guess what theme it was? If you said nature, your right. So they set up the party.

They added animal balloons, food, plants, and other nature things to their party. Suddenly, the leader of a nature group who was helping hang bird feeders that were protective got an idea. Can you guess what the idea was?

(Written September 2016 at 14-years-old)

SPREADING THE GREAT NATURE

Did you guess the right answer?

As the leader wrote special invitations, the leader of the nature group suggested "I got an awesome idea. How about we spread the great nature? Would you spread the news to our good nature-loving friends with the invitations?"

The group responded "That's a great idea. Let's make it happen! Sure, we would love to spread the news." So the rest of the group set out to spread the news.

The group leader began to spread the nature. After the group leader began, the leader waited for the rest of her group to spread the nature the rest of the day. The group worked all day and all night every day and every night.

Can you guess what the nature group did after they spread the great nature?

(Written September 2016 at 15-years-old)

THE BIG DAY FOR NATURE

The nature team prepared for the party. Meanwhile, Nature chatted about the party made just for them. They were all excited.

"I'm so excited." said the eldest bird. "The nature party will be held at 1:00 p.m. The time is 12:50 p.m. right now. Shall we be on our way?" said the wisest old tree. All the nature things including the trees and bird said, "Yes, we should be on our way. I agree."

So off they went to the nature party. When they arrived, their eyes were wide open with shock and surprise from what they saw. Can you imagine what they saw?

(Written October 2016 at 15-years-old)

WHAT THE ANIMALS SAW

The animals saw incredible nature decorations and their eyes got wide open from seeing such majestic detailed decorations. "Let the party begin!" exclaimed the nature team who helped organize such a wondrous and thriving party.

All the nature things said, "Yes, let the party begin." All the nature things cheered and whooped. The animals sang while the trees danced. At 3:00 p.m. precisely, they had a special visitor come to their extravaganza nature party.

Why did the nature things cheer? Why did the animals sing while the trees danced? Who was the special visitor?

(Written October 2016 at 15-years-old)

THE SURPRISES

The nature animals and plants cheered with excitement for the nature party that began. The animals sang while the trees danced because they were excited. The special visitor was a unicorn and a special fairy called the Life and Nature Fairy.

The nature things asked, "Why is a unicorn with Life and Nature Fairy here? Is there a reason?" The fairy said, "I'm here because I've heard about this unique nature party. I've heard about the party from my good friend the Animal Fairy and I've come to help you get some more people to hear about this lovely party."

"I'm glad you think our party is unique and lovely. We certainly could use more attention," said the nature party leader. So the Nature Fairy set off to find some people, fairies, princesses, fantasy animals, and mermaids.

One by one, the guests began to arrive. What did the guests do when they got there?

(Written October 2016 at 15-years-old)

WHAT THE GUESTS DID AT THE PARTY

The party guests were very pleased that the unicorn and the Nature Fairy came to their incredible party so they made the unicorn and the Nature Fairy the guests of honor.

The Nature Fairy said, "I really must go to get you more attention for your nature party. I really enjoyed being the guest of honor and my unicorn said that she enjoyed being the animal of honor."

As she spoke kindly, she got ready to go find some people who would be inspired, impressed, and most importantly have fun at the party. Meanwhile, the nature party leader decided to make better expressions so the guests rode their animals and had a race. They also set up games, entertainment, and more.

The Nature Fairy found some great people who are willing to give the Nature party a try. She also found polar seals, tiger dog, and other fantasy animals.

(Written November 2016 at 15-years-old)

POEMS AND SONGS

NOTEBOOK

N is for Nature

O is for Outstanding

T is for Terrific

E is for Eager Writing

B is for Book

O is for Outrageous

O is for Ocean

K is for Kindness

(Written May 2017 at 15-years-old)

TRIPLE POEMS

Hey, everyone! I've decided to put together three poems for you to read. I got inspired by "Leap Into Poetry" by Avis Harley. I hope you enjoy!

Alliteration:

Moons meet mountains.

Simile:

The sun rises like a bright flashlight.
The moon rises like a beaming light.
The sun sets as a wink in the sky.
The moon sets as a vanilla cookie in the
awakening sky.

Riddle:

I'm awake in the nighttime.
I sleep during the daytime light.
I watch the sunset and the sunrise every day
and night.

Can you guess who I am?
(bird)

Yes-No Poem (Just answer yes or no to the questions):

Are sunsets colorful?
Are sunrises beautiful?
Are sunsets breathtaking?
Are sunrises full of color?
Do sunsets and sunrises rise and set at the same time?

(Written October 2016 at 15-years-old)

SHADOWS ARE ALWAYS THERE

Shadows are the darkness of day.
Shadows are the eclipses of the day.
Shadows are almost always there.
Shadows are fast as a cheetah.
Shadows are entertaining like a prism.
Shadows are bright like a rainbow.

Shadows are from the sun.
Shadows are from the super moon.
Shadows are from the bright stars.
Shadows are awesome.
Shadows are funny.
Shadows appear everywhere at one point.

(Written September 2015 at 13-years-old)

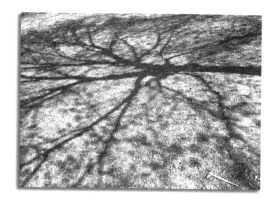

ENCHANTED EGYPTIAN BEAUTY

Triangular prisms sprout rainbows
From the tip of a triangle, triangles peak
everywhere
Amazing colorful teeth pointing toward a
catchy circle
It is an Egyptian Beauty!

(Written May 2016 at 14-years-old)

A FRIENDLY LETTER TO ROBERT FROST

Hey there, Robert Frost!

I had no idea that you live in New Hampshire. I loved your winter poems and some of the other poems you wrote. I hope you love New Hampshire! I've heard it's beautiful there!

I like poetry and I know you like reading because you are technically an author. Take your time to read this. Enjoy a nice day!

Best wishes,
Lillian

P.S. My family says hello.

(Written July 2015 at 13-years-old)

"Dust of Snow"
by Robert Frost

The way a crow
Shook down on me
The dust of snow
From a hemlock tree
Has given my heart
A change of mood
And saved some part
Of a day I had rued.

LOVE IS MAGICAL

Cows are loud and can moo
sometimes they say,
I love you!

Cows have milk,
and cows eat grass.

You are surrounded by love
every breath you take is love
You are love

Guinea pigs wheek and guinea pigs meek,
lovey dovey guinea piggy moo!

Love is the butterfly
gracefully it flies
magical is its color

Love is magical
the alchemy of peace.

Airplanes flying
through the air
fun galore!

How beautiful the bird flies,
as the wind.

Love is the tree
Love is the flower
Love is the silence.

Flowers blossom
pollen falls.

Rainbow is the sky
Rainbow is the water
Rainbow is the colors of the earth.

Nature is love
Nature knows how to be.

Team TLC
always kind
always thinking.

Kindness is always there
Kindness is like friendship

A wise man
is kind to the kind
and kind to the unkind

A wise man
under a tree

Blue bird flies to Alaska
Red bird flies to Hawaii
White bird flies to Australia

The magical hummingbird
arrives on a warm summer day

Sushi
best food ever
try some

Pineapple
Most delicious food ever

Mindful eating
Mindful living
The way of peace and happiness

Eating is fun
and yummy

Apple trees grow with sunshine
Butterflies grow with food
Cake gets eaten fast or slow.

Beings, trees, and insects
We are all one love.

(Written July 2015 at 13-years-old)

Team TLC (Thomas, Lillian, and Camilla) wrote this Renga poem. It took us about one to two weeks as the nature of a Renga is that authors take turns writing a stanza.

Renga: (as defined by Poets.org)

"Renga, meaning "linked poem," began over seven hundred years ago in Japan to encourage the collaborative composition of poems. Poets worked in pairs or small groups, taking turns composing the alternating three-line and two-line stanzas.

In order for the poem to achieve its trajectory, each poet writes a new stanza that leaps from only the stanza preceding it. This leap advances both the thematic movement as well as maintaining the linking component.

Contemporary practitioners of Renga have eased the form's traditional structural standards, allowing poets to adjust line-length, while still offering exciting and enlightening possibilities."

IN THE GOOD OLE SUMMERTIME – LILLIAN'S VERSION

Chorus:

In the good ole summertime
In the good ole summertime

(Repeat Chorus x1)

We used to eat summer food
We used to eat summer food
Go to bed early
Go to bed early

(Repeat Chorus x2)

Go to bed early in the good ole summertime.
Go to bed early in the good ole summertime.

(Written June 2015 at 13-years-old)

FLOWER POEM

Pretty flowers are finally here.

Pink flowers bloom so elegant
And they grow leaves.

White flowers bloom ever so gracefully
And they give food.

Yellow flowers bloom nicely
And they give smell.

Purple flowers bloom slowly
And they give beauty.

Red flowers bloom fast
And they give color.

Blue flowers bloom in spring
And they give scent.

(Written March 2015 at 13-years-old)

MERRY CHRISTMAS

Aloha Christmas!
Aloha Christmas!
Aloha Thanksgiving!
Aloha Thanksgiving!
My how the year has gone by faster than
I expected ever known.
My how the year has gone by faster than I
expected.
Aloha Christmas!
Aloha Christmas!
Aloha Thanksgiving!
Aloha Thanksgiving-giving!

(Written December 2014 at 13-years-old)

A COLOR POEM

Red smells like fresh pine.
Orange smells like oranges.
Yellow smells like fruit.
Green smells like trees.
Blue smells like water.
Purple smells like plum.

(Written March 2014 at 12-years-old)

ABCS OF FOOD

A – Awesome Apple

B – Batty Bananas

C – Crazy Carrots

D – Delicious Donut

E – Eager Eggs

F – Freaky Fries

G – Good Ginger

H – Hyper Hash Browns

I – Icy Ice Cream

J – Jumpy Jello

K – Kooky Kiwi

L – Loopy Lollipop

M – Merry Mango

N – Nutty Nectarines

O – Outstanding Olives

P – Perky Pear

Q – Quirky Quinoa

R – Red Radish

S – Snoopy Strawberry

T – Tricky Taco

U – Useful Ugli

V – Violet Vegetables

W – Working Waffles

X – Xeric Xacutti

Y – Yellow Yams

Z – Zany Zucchini

(Written March 2014 at 12-years-old)

ACROSTIC POEM FOR EASTER

Eager Eggs
Awesome Apples
Super Strawberry
Tranquil Turkey Burgers
Exciting Elderberry
Remarkable Roast Beef

Bountiful Broccoli
Useful Ugli
Nice Nuts
Neat Nectarine
Yellow Squash

(Written March 2014 at 12-years-old)

EASTER POEMS

E is for Exciting
A is for Awesome

S is for Sunny
T is for Tranquil
E is for Eager
R is for Remarkable

A: An Easter girl hops on a stone.
B: Beautiful girl she was.
C: Chameleon is out and is turning red.
D: Dandelion is enjoying the weather.

The Easter Day is nice
A feaster hay is peace
May lester stay, Liz mice!
Easter
Sunny, Spring

Flowers Bloom
Happy, Likes Birds
Holiday

Blue feels like an ocean.
Blue tastes like blueberry.
Blue looks like a pool.
Blue smells like berry.
Blue sounds like a fan.

(Written March 2014 at 12-years-old)

WHAT AM I POEMS

Rhyming/What Am I Poem

It is only seen in fairy tales.
It is tonly been in tairy bales.
It is bonly teen tin bairy whales.
What Am I?

I am a preteen and I'm writing.
What am I?

(unicorn & I Jillian)

(Written March 2014 at 12-years-old)

A RIDDLE – A POET POEM

Do you love riddles? This just might be the riddle for you!

What do poets do for fun?

(Poetry)

(Written March 2014 at 12-years-old)

TEAM TLC ROCKS

T is for Talent which we do have a lot of talents in this "team".
E is for Enthusiasm which means we have excitement around us sometimes.
A is for Awesome which Team TLC is awesome.

M is for Melody or Music which we have melody and music in Team TLC.

T is for Team and of course we are a team or else it would just be the letters "T, L, and C". **L** is for Laughter which we do have a lot of laughing.
C is Calm which we do have calmness.

R is for Respect which we do respect each other.
O is for Outside which we go outside.
C is for Cheerful which we are often cheerful.
K is for Kindness which we do have.
S is for Strong which our membership keeps together with.

(Written March 2014 at 12-years-old)

NEVADA DAY

I like living in Nevada because usually there are birds tweeting 'bout, and bright sunshine peeking above, and so much sights to see and do.

N is for Nevada Sights
E is for Eva Adams
V is for Vehicles
A is for Andre Agassi
D is for Dates with Camilla
A is for Abby Dalton

D is for Dat-So-La-Lee
A is for Adolph Sutro
Y is for H.M. Yerington

Nevada is the greatest place to live because I love doing things here in Reno and Sparks; and there are many experiences to make.

(Written October 2012 at 11-years-old)

A SONG CALLED SNOW SNOW

Snow
Snow
Snow is the best thing.
Snow
Snow
Snow, I love you!
Snow
Snow
To my dearest brother, Thomas.

(Written February 2012 at 10-years-old)

MUMMY POEM

Your my mummy
I love you so much
thin to my head,
I like your French Fries.

(Written December 2011 at 10-years-old)

HALLOWEEN POEM

Black cats cross the street
Black bats fly across the street
White ghost scare the people
Striped candy corn gets eaten
People wear famous costumes
Happy jack-o-lanterns watch as they smile
Happy Halloween

(Written October 2011 at 10-years-old)

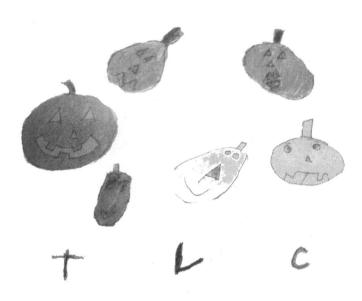

MY SHOE

My shoe has grew bamboo,
My sock got walked over by a woman.
My feet has a tweet,
My shoe has grew bamboo.

(Written August 2011 at 9-years-old)

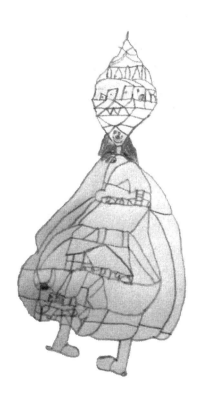

PRETTY FLOWERS

A poem is a sweet brainer.
You listen to music.
And the point is that your
Creative brain is a bank.
And listen to it.
I love you a lot, of pretty flowers.

(Written April 2011 at 9-years-old)

HAPPINESS

Life is so happy, it makes me cry.
And I cannot, tell a lie on April Fools.
The point is that you will have a nonstop
lovable brain.
And it has our choices in it.

(Written April 2011 at 9-years-old)

CLOSING

May you always live your life as if it's your very own fairy tale. Because it is! I'd like to share some of my favorite quotes with you.

"A blank piece of paper is God's way of telling us how hard it is be God." - Sidney Shelton

"Not that the story need be long, but it will take a while to make it short." - Henry David Thoreau

"If music be food of love, play on." - William Shakespeare

"Life itself is the most wonderful fairy tale." - Hans Christian Andersen

"Look deep into nature, and then you will understand everything better." - Albert Einstein

"Autumn is a second spring when every leaf is a flower." - Albert Camus

"Nature always wears the colors of the spirit." - Ralph Waldo Emerson

"The mountains are calling and I must go." - John Muir

"But they say if you dream a thing more than once, it's sure to come true." - Walt Disney Company

"Live each day as if your life had just begun." - Johann Wolfgang Von Goethe

"We become what we think about." - Earl Nightingale

"The mind is everything. What you think you become." - Buddha

"Always wear your invisible crown." – Unknown

Lillian Darnell

ABOUT THE AUTHOR

Lillian Darnell

Lillian Darnell is sixteen-years-old and this is her debut book. She is unschooled; which is similar to homeschooling and means that she focuses on her interests and talents with learning. Lillian loves to draw, paint, read, write, track the weather, and enjoys being in nature. She has a chromosome difference simply called 18p- which affects 1 in 56,000 people.

"Laughing is the sunshine of your heart." - Lillian

Lillian and her mother have a date day together once a month that began when she was a toddler. Also, Team TLC has a weekly movie night, usually on Saturday, that began when Lillian was a toddler. Some of her favorite foods are French fries, cheese, dark chocolate, snickerdoodle cookies, chocolate cake, and strawberries. Lillian really enjoys volunteering at the South Valleys Library one day a week. She lives with her family of authors in Reno, Nevada.

You can learn more about Lillian at her website: LillianDarnell.com.

CONTRIBUTING EDITOR AND AUTHOR

Camilla Downs

Camilla Downs is Lillian's mother and she is extremely excited for Lillian that this book has finally come to be. She is a mom, bestselling author, writer, blogger, poet, and nature photographer. Some of her favorite topics and practices are meditating, mindfulness, and emotional connection. Camilla loves being with her two kids, creating adventures, reading, going for walks, connecting with nature, volunteering at the library and the Humane Society, and sharing all of this with others. She lives with her two kids, Thomas and Lillian, in Reno, Nevada.

Camilla's first book, *"D iz for Different - One Woman's Journey to Acceptance"*, published in 2012 reached #1 in Special Needs Parenting and #2 in Self-Help on Amazon. You can learn more about Camilla at her website and other social media outlets:

CamillaDowns.com
facebook.com/CamillaDowns
instagram.com/CamillaDowns

CONTRIBUTING EDITOR

Thomas Darnell

Thomas Darnell is twelve-years-old. He is also unschooled and some of his favorite topics are Minecraft, LEGOS, coding, and math. He enjoys Fibonacci numbers, Bernoulli's equation, and the law of infinite probability. Some of his most cherished things to do are reading, being outside, going on adventures, and swimming.

Thomas and his mother have a date day together once a month that began when he was a toddler. Thomas loves volunteering at the Nevada Humane Society one day a week in the cat rooms. He lives with his family of authors in Reno, Nevada.

Thomas' first book, *"Biggest Little Photographer"*, was published in October 2016. As an eight-year-old he took a picture a day for 365 days of a LEGO mini-figure taking a picture; which was later made into a book. The book carries a message that life is what happens from here to there, what happens between deciding what you want, and receiving that which you want.

You can learn more about Thomas at his website: ThomasADarnell.com

TEAM Thomas Lillian Camilla

You can follow Team TLC adventures on their website and blog at: TheTeamTLC.com.

The Chromosome 18 Registry & Research Society is a lay advocacy organization composed primarily of individuals with a chromosome 18 abnormality. We consist of three separate organizations located in the United States, Australia, and Europe, all with a common mission: To help people with chromosome 18 abnormalities overcome the obstacles they face so they may lead happy, healthy, and productive lives. We are proud to count among our members those who are affected by a chromosome 18 abnormality, extended family members, and professionals. Membership is open to any interested person. We are a 501(c)(3) non-profit, tax-exempt public charity.

Our work is supported by memberships and donations from individuals and charitable organizations. We have met the strict criteria for fiscal responsibility set by the Combined Federal Campaign.

Identifying Treatments for Chromosome 18 Conditions

The Chromosome 18 Clinical Research Center is dedicated to understanding chromosome 18 conditions and to developing treatments. This is a long process. We must collect data on the natural history of the chromosome 18 conditions; identify the key genes responsible for those features; and identify drugs that can regulate those genes. With the help of families with chromosome 18 conditions, The Research Center has already made great progress towards our goals.

The Chromosome 18
Registry & Research Society

Information courtesy of The Chromosome 18 Registry & Research Society. To learn more visit Chromosome18.org.

When Lillian's mother, Camilla, asked me if I could help with the layout and design of Lillian's book I jumped at the chance. I had followed Lillian's blog for some time and cherished her insightful fresh voice and deeply enchanting view of life. Lillian's words are wise and wonderful, fanciful and true. I have loved being immersed in Lillian's world, and I'm so blessed and honored to have been a part of this project! With thanks, ~ Kate Raina, graphic design

To contact me, feel free to visit at:

www.kateraina.crevado.com
www.behance.net/Kate_Raina
kate_raina@yahoo.com

"The sun shines beautifully as you." - Lillian Darnell

Made in the USA
Middletown, DE
28 February 2018